BEZI

C000162885

Biographer, novelist, playwright, an[...] SYMONDS (1914-2006) was the illeg[...] expert Robert Wemyss Symonds an[...] gate. Coming to London at sixteen, he educated himself in the British Museum reading room and became part of the writerly scene in Soho. Acquainted with Orwell and Dylan Thomas (whose wife once tried to stab him) he worked for *Picture Post* and edited the magazine *Lilliput*. His novels include *Light Over Water* (1963), about a young female guru in South London, and *The Guardian of the Threshold* (1980), also esoterically themed, but his most popular fictions were books for children such as *Elfrida and the Pig* (1959), illustrated by Edward Ardizzone. He also wrote *Conversations with Gerald* (1974), an exceptional memoir of Gerald Hamilton, the original for Isherwood's Mr. Norris, but nothing else enjoyed such sensational success as his Aleister Crowley biography *The Great Beast*.

John Symonds

BEZILL

A Novel

with a new introduction by
PHIL BAKER

VALANCOURT BOOKS

Bezill by John Symonds
First published in Great Britain by The Unicorn Press in 1962
First Valancourt Books edition 2022

Published by Valancourt Books, Richmond, Virginia
http://www.valancourtbooks.com

ISBN 978-1-954321-65-6 (trade paperback)
Also available as an electronic book.

Cover art by Val Biro, restored by M.S. Corley
Set in Bembo Book MT Pro

Introduction

Doomed to be remembered largely as the biographer of twentieth-century magus Aleister Crowley, self-appointed Beast 666 and "wickedest man in the world", John Symonds was a writer of far greater range than that might suggest. Along with a couple of other biographies he wrote delightful children's books such as *The Magic Currant Bun*, uncompromisingly uncommercial stage plays, and some subtle and atmospheric novels—the greatest of them perhaps his 1962 *Bezill*.

A delicately Gothic fiction that cries out to have been illustrated by Edward Gorey, *Bezill* is a book about the mysteries of sex. It is also very funny, once the reader becomes attuned to it, and ultimately rather moving. *Bezill* is the story of Geoffrey Pellerin, who takes a job at a remote mansion in the English countryside—Bezill Tower—as tutor to young Herbert, the boy of the house. In particular, Herbert's mother wants her son to be instructed in the facts of life: the birds and the bees, "nature", and perhaps even *sol* and *luna*, the sun and moon; "quite a lecture on alchemy", as Pellerin thinks of his own rather esoteric attempts to explain it all.

It is, in other words, a book about the strange question of what adults get up to, a subject that circles around what Freud called the "primal scene": the child's dark and haunting intuition of parental sex sensed as something over the horizon, leaving scattered hints and clues like a detective story. And in parallel with Herbert's initiation into these ritual mysteries, in larger counterpart, comes the mystery for Pellerin himself of exactly what it is that Herbert's mother—Mrs Shakeshaft—and her companion Mr Gayfere get up to. Pellerin can't help wondering if it is "some awful secret", and all the more awful because he finds himself in love with Mrs Shakeshaft. As the previous tutor, Chauncey—departing under a cloud for some reason, and briefly encountered by Pellerin at the railway station—tells him vaguely, whatever it is, "It usually goes on in her bedroom."

English humour is known for its tendency to innuendo, popularly associated with the *Carry On* comedy films such as *Carry On Nurse* (so much so, that the catching of a double entendre, particularly unintentional, is now traditionally met with cries of "Ooh, Matron!"). There is no shortage of these winking and nudging moments in *Bezill*, right from Chauncey's early observation that at Bezill "they mount you once a fortnight" (he is talking about horse riding). And why, as the story progresses, does Gayfere sit on a rubber cushion? And what, wonders Pellerin, is really at the (uh) "bottom of their relationship"?

Remembering German sexologist Krafft-Ebing (author of the *Psychopathia Sexualis*, his notorious 1886 compendium of case histories, latterly illustrated by Robert Crumb) and Havelock Ellis, among others, Pellerin reflects that the facts of life are a vast area: straightforward sex is large enough, and the curious avenues of perversity even larger. But the down-to-earth Mrs Shakeshaft—a fox-hunting enthusiast who wears jackboots and has never been seen with a book, "only a riding crop"—doesn't want him getting lost in details. He realizes she just wants him to stick, perhaps appropriately, to the "rudiments".

Rudiments notwithstanding, the *Bezill* setting is finely atmospheric. There is a typically bygone country railway station (with a slow train moving no faster than a bus);

ivy on the walls of Bezill Tower, outside the stained glass windows; and stuffed birds, along with a pike from 1911, preserved in the hermetic world of their glass cases ("ivory towers within ivory towers, worlds within worlds"). Like the Mortmere of Edward Upward's *The Railway Accident and Other Stories*, the remote domain of Bezill is itself a dated and parodic English world with a quietly surreal atmosphere, forming the backdrop for Symonds' knowing Gothic touches. Not only is there a locked tower (associated in this case with a mad aunt) but a cellar—that classic topos of gothic psychology—with a heavy key. "She wanted him to tell Herbert about the facts of life," thinks Pellerin, "Was that why she'd given him the key to the wine cellar? Could there be a connection?"

The players in this miniature Gothic drama are notable for their barely natural names, entwined with curious meanings. Pellerin is a pilgrim, come to this house of strange new experience, met by the driver Fulalove. The name of Mrs Shakeshaft is more innuendo-laden, suggesting a subject supposedly as English as innuendo itself ("Got any straight sex, then?" a man asks in Gillian Freeman's classic study of erotica in the 1960s, *The Undergrowth of Literature*: "Sorry mate," says the man behind the counter in the Soho bookshop, "it's all got a bit of fladge in it.") Gayfere's name is even more heavily loaded with meaning, and in uncertain directions: he's a "queer fish, a text-book case" says Chauncey of this rather repressed character, and there are vague, inexplicit notes sounded about Corvo, Gide, Taormina, and "urnings", while at the same time a straightforward mention of Oscar Wilde makes Gayfere shudder: "he had, apparently, an abhorrence of Wilde."

These are rare surnames, and it is possible Symonds found inspiration by flicking through the London *"A to Z"*. Chancing to walk through Gayfere Road (SW1), I wondered if any others figured in the street directory, and there are indeed Pellerin Road (N16), Chauncey Street (N9), and Pasquier—name of a minor character—in Pasquier Road (E17). Bezill itself remains mysterious, a Continental name that occurs fleetingly in mediaeval England, but it is perhaps further suggestive of Beelzebub (or for that matter Beelzy, as in John Collier's celebrated short story of 1940, "Thus I Refute Beelzy").

The name of Herbert has a resonance all its own. It is now a rather endearing name, in the way that dated names easily become sentimental: a suitable name for a pet frog or a tortoise, perhaps. But when Symonds was writing, it also had an odd life as a name associated with youth and trouble; someone delinquent might be a "right Herbert" and Herberts might slash the seats in cinemas. It is this youthful sense of the name that is preserved in the 1961 film *Espresso Bongo*, featuring teenage music star "Bongo Herbert".

Whatever the name meant to Symonds, poor sensitive Herbert—who is prone to fits and recoils from being "blooded" with a freshly killed fox, in another distinctive initiation—is the book's most memorable character. He seems to be the product of a dark secret in the family's past, and the generally sexualized atmosphere of the book inevitably colours his description: we are told young Herbert has "dark shadows under his eyes" as if he has hardly slept—he has masturbatory eyes—and if that sounds like an over-reading on its first appearance, it is confirmed a few chapters later when "purple rings" around his eyes suggest to Pellerin that nightly "succubi" might be "draining away his manhood". He is pallid and short (he might in fact have stunted his growth, as the cliché has it) but at the same time "quite good-looking in bed" (as the text innocently puts it, simply talking about height: "for then one didn't know how short he was").

8

The mystery of human relationships is also a central feature in some of Symonds' other books. "Don't refuse love", a character is told in the climactic final line of his more metropolitan and gloomily farcical novel *The Only Thing That Matters*: "Why, it's the only thing that matters." But it is only in the present novel that it reaches such well-turned thematic perfection, or becomes quite as emotionally affecting as the growing friendship between Pellerin and Herbert, while Pellerin is embarking on his ill-fated attempts to conduct Herbert's *éducation sentimentale*.

At first Pellerin imagines them walking in country lanes, talking of flowers and poetry, and this in turn gives way to more solidly focused ideas of visiting Pompei to see the frescoes, or going to Naples for the Eroticum Neapolitanum. At last it all solidifies into the start of a Grand Tour-like trip to Europe ("He told Herbert of the wonderful portraits by Velazquez of court dwarfs and fantastic sketches of witches and succubi by Goya in the Prado") ending in a Portuguese brothel where he attempts to introduce Herbert as a young English milord. We last encounter Herbert as Pellerin is leaving Bezill—like his predecessor, sacked and under a cloud—and Herbert rushes out in front of the car he is being driven in. He manages to halt it, to say goodbye: "I shall miss you," he says. "And I you, Herbert," says Pellerin.

Thomas De Quincey's *Confessions of an English Opium Eater* has a famous inset story in which young De Quincey and the child prostitute who befriends him, Ann, lose each other near Oxford Street and never meet again. When De Quincey's *Confessions* were translated by the French poet Alfred de Musset he seems to have found this story so sad that, extraordinarily, he takes bizarre liberties with translation and simply writes Ann back into the story for a reunion. I have to confess to my own de Musset moment when I think of *Bezill*, and the parting of our two main characters.

Any speculations on what happens, outside the actual text of a work, necessarily takes us into the notorious realm of wondering what Lady Macbeth was doing ten minutes before the play began; but no matter. I have to know that Pellerin and Herbert will meet again one day, and I am sure they do.

PHIL BAKER
February 14, 2022

Phil Baker's books include *The Devil is a Gentleman: The Life and Times of Dennis Wheatley*, and *Austin Osman Spare: The Life and Legend of London's Lost Artist*. He has also written an academic book on Samuel Beckett and a cultural history of absinthe, and edited a collection of essays on Fu Manchu creator Sax Rohmer. He lives in London, reviews for several papers including the *Times Literary Supplement*, and has an interest in the byways of popular and not so popular culture.

I

The train from London stopped at a small station in an eastern county of England, and several passengers got out. With the exception of one passenger—who was carrying a suitcase and a portable typewriter—they all made for the exit and disappeared. After a moment or two of hesitation, the passenger with the suitcase and the typewriter also made for the exit, but only to ask the ticket collector who was standing there a question.

"Can you tell me," he said, "when the train for Windwood arrives?"

The ticket collector glanced at a list pinned up in his sentry-box. "At four fifteen, sir," he replied.

"But it's not yet three o'clock."

After a moment of thought, the ticket collector said, "Yes, you've got a bit of a wait, sir."

The train he had arrived on began to move off. The carriages were fairly full. Well, he was glad, at least, that he had got off that train, and wasn't being carried on to goodness-only knows where. Then the grim thought arose that he was going to a place equally, if not more, obscure, along a branch line which, for all he could see, hadn't yet been built.

"Where do I get this train when it arrives?"

"At platform two, sir."

"Thank you." He picked up his suitcase and retreated along the platform.

It was an autumn day, sunny and warm, not a day to be regretful about anything.

He had one and a quarter hours to wait. On the other side of the railway track was a small private enclosure stuffed with trees. Their leaves were yellow and brown and thinning out. In the tallest trees were big nests, rooks' nests, deserted now.

They will come back next year, he thought, before the leaves have sprouted again, remake and reline their nests, lay like mad.

And would he, Geoffrey Pellerin, return in the spring? Yes, his appointment was for six months only; at the end of it he could go back home. It was a dead-end job he was going to, anyhow.

The after-effects of a cold made him feel like using his handkerchief. Instead he spat over the edge of the platform.

His employer, Mrs Shakeshaft, whom he had not yet met, was disappointed when he declined a contract for a year.

He got up to see where his spittle had landed: on a sleeper. He gazed at it for a whole minute, his mind filled with unquiet thoughts about his future; then he returned to the bench.

No, no! Six months was long enough to tutor an ailing, backward boy. Besides, the boy might die before the spring.

He did not know the nature of his pupil's complaint. He hoped it wasn't anything catching, like consumption. Mrs Shakeshaft hadn't told him, and he hadn't asked.

He wouldn't be tutoring at all, running the terrible risks of boredom and of catching consumption (or whatever the boy suffered from in the way of a catching complaint) if it weren't for Gladys.

Gladys dispelled all other thoughts. First, the image of her—her brown hair and brown eyes and full lips, lips suggestive of sensuality, but which, curiously, were without any sensuality, chaste lips in fact. She was several years older than Pellerin. A river flowing swiftly to the falls. They'd been lovers for a time; then they'd broken apart, but only to come together again. She wanted, he knew, to get married. He did not want to get married, not yet anyhow, and not to Gladys—and yet it was Gladys that he felt he should marry, if anyone, and Gladys knew this.

To end the conflict, he'd written to Ditchend and Swatman, the educational agents, asking them to find him a post as a resident tutor. He must get away, not too far away, but a hundred miles away at least. Messrs Ditchend and Swatman had sent him a short list of vacant posts. He'd applied for two of them, and been accepted by Mrs Shakeshaft, and without any prior interview. (Did she, he wondered, want a tutor for her boy so badly that she didn't care what he looked like?)

"I want to think about us!" he'd said, when he'd told Gladys, the flowing river, of what he'd done.

The arrival of a train interrupted further thoughts. Pellerin got up and seized his belongings. Could this be his train? It was stopping at platform two. The ticket collector suddenly reappeared. Pellerin hurried up to him.

"No, not your train," he said, anticipating the question. "It's come from where you want to go to."

Pellerin relaxed and turned away. He wandered back to the bench and sat down again. He glanced at a short, square man with plump cheeks who was emerging from one of the two first-class carriages. He was about Pellerin's age, that is to say in his early twenties, but unlike Pellerin he'd found time to develop an angry, rather fierce, expression.

He threw his two suitcases on to the platform, paced his racquet on top of them, glanced about. Then he looked at Pellerin.

Pellerin cast his eyes to the ground. It was embarrassing to be caught in that fierce gaze. He heard footsteps approaching; then a voice saying:

"Can you tell me when the train to London comes in?"

The voice fitted the man.

Pellerin looked up. "I'm afraid I can't," he replied. "I'm not going there myself." He got up.

He was wearing, Pellerin saw, an Old Harrovian tie—two narrow diagonal white lines on a blue background—and on his plump cheeks was the fringe of a beard, too high for the razor to reach, Pellerin supposed.

He was taller than this Old Harrovian, but not so broad across the shoulders. "I'm going in the other direction," he said, "to Windwood."

Why had he said this? Was it due to an intuition that the Old Harrovian had come from there?

The glaring, angry look which had faded from the Old Harrovian's face returned in full strength.

"To Windwood?" he said. He glanced at Pellerin's suitcase and typewriter. "You're not by any chance going to Bezill Tower?" The name of the house he pronounced with sarcasm. Did he, Pellerin wondered, detest the people there?

"As a matter of fact, I am," he said. "Is there a tower?"

"Surprisingly, there is," said the Old Harrovian. "A stunted tower." He looked at Pellerin thoughtfully, as if trying to make up his mind about something. "Are you the new tutor?" There was a trace of disgust in his voice.

"Yes, I am," said Pellerin modestly. He felt uncomfortable, wished he'd not spoken to this man, wished he could vanish into thin air. But they'd been drawn to each other. Two tutors on a deserted country railway platform, the one going, the other returning. He wanted to tell him why he'd turned tutor. Because of Gladys. A means of escape. Think of me as yourself going there. How will I fare? Are they nice people?

"I don't envy you," said the Old Harrovian. He was

14

silent for a moment. "The food's jolly good and they mount you once a fortnight."

"Ah," said Pellerin with a relieved expression as if he'd been told some good news. They mount you . . . What exactly? . . . Of course. But he didn't ride. Still, the outlook was promising.

"There's a man called Gayfere there," continued the Old Harrovian. "He's a queer fish, a text-book case if you ask me. He claims to have known Baron Corvo, and almost every interesting writer since, but I think he's a liar."

"What's Mrs Shakeshaft like?" Pellerin waited keenly for his answer.

"Haven't you met her?"

"No, my appointment was arranged by Ditchend and Swatman. She was too busy."

"She wasn't for me." He was thoughtful for a moment; then he said, "She's as cold as a fish, and under the thumb of Percy Gayfere."

"Oh, I see, he's her . . ."

"No." The Old Harrovian shook his head.

"Mr Shakeshaft?"

"Dead."

"May I ask your name?" said Pellerin.

"It seems superfluous to tell you my name. I shall always be one jump ahead of you. However, you are bound to hear of me sooner or later at Bezill Tower. Gayfere will tell you." And in a squeaky voice, he added: "We had a horrible fellow here to teach Herbert called Henry Chauncy. He was a bad influence."

"In what way?" said Pellerin, smiling.

"Morally," replied Chauncy with a severe look.

"Oh, dear," said Pellerin, laughing.

Chauncy began to smile.

"I'm sure he'll say the same of me when I've left," said

Pellerin, wishing he could take a razor and remove the patches of beard on Chauncy's cheek-bones.

"Not for the same reason, I hope," replied Chauncy. He was frowning now. There was a moment or two of silence. "Look," said Chauncy, "since you're going to take my place, there's something I should like you to do for me. I'll give you my address." He took out his wallet, and extracted from it a small white card. Hurriedly he wrote on it, and gave it to Pellerin. "There's a fine looking girl there—a maid. She's called Beatrice and comes from St Helena. When you see her you'll agree with me . . ."

He stopped to glance at a train which was drawing in.

"About what?" asked Pellerin, anxious to know all.

"That it was worth getting chucked out because of her," continued Chauncy. He laughed lightly and bitterly. "She's got a drop of negro blood, I think."

"That's not my train, I suppose?" said Pellerin with agitated gesture.

"No, I think it's mine," replied Chauncy. "It's not going to Windwood, anyhow. Now, I want you to do this for me." He picked up one of his suitcases. "I shall write to her, but I feel that she won't write to me. Some people just *don't* write, and not because they don't know how to write or don't want to write."

"What do you want me to do?" asked Pellerin anxiously.

Chauncy put his tennis racquet under his arm and took hold of his other suitcase. "I want you to do this," he said, coming at last to the point. "I want you to write and tell me about her,—if she's unhappy, I mean."

It was now clear that the train which had just come in was going to London.

"But how shall I know if she's unhappy?" said Pellerin with a puzzled, worried look. Was he, he wondered, supposed to grow intimate with this girl, know of her every mood?

Chauncy shrugged his shoulders at this needless objection. He moved across the platform. Pellerin followed. Chauncy took hold of a carriage door handle, and opened the door. He put his luggage inside.

A door slammed; then another. His was the only door open.

"What's worrying you?" he asked.

After this remark, pride made Pellerin decline to say. "I thought you were going to tell me some awful secret about Mrs Shakeshaft and Mr Whatshisname."

"I can if you wish."

Chauncy got into the carriage. He wasn't going to be left on the platform. He closed the door. Pellerin looked helplessly at him through the glass. There was a man wearing a bowler hat in the carriage with Chauncy. He looked up from *The Times*.

Chauncy lowered the window and leaned out.

"Thank you for agreeing to write to me about Beatrice—a lovely girl."

"But what about?" demanded Pellerin.

"If there's anything to write about you'll know," replied Chauncy mysteriously.

"You were going to tell me about Mrs Shakeshaft," said Pellerin desperately. A whistle sounded.

"It's about Gayfere. He's . . ." Chauncy hesitated. "Oh, you'd better find out for yourself." He began to laugh in a helpless way, as if what he was thinking was terribly funny.

"Find out *what*?"

"It usually goes on in her bedroom."

The train began to move.

"What does?" shouted Pellerin desperately.

Chauncy made a movement with his right hand like someone playing tennis. He was now receding fast. "Goodbye!" he shouted. And he began to laugh again.

Pellerin's gesture indicated that he was being left hopelessly in the dark.

Only Chauncy's laughing face was visible. It created such a strong impression on Pellerin that he could still see it after the train had vanished.

"He'll always be one jump ahead of me," he said, shaking his head; he looked disconsolately at the card he was holding in his hand. *Mr Henry Chauncy* was engraved in the centre of it, and underneath, in biro ink, was written an address in Oakley Street, Chelsea.

2

This part of the journey reminded Pellerin of a bus ride in town; the train was certainly going no faster than a bus.

He was alone in the narrow old-fashioned carriage which went well, he thought, with the old-fashioned train. The view was pleasant enough: autumn woods and ivy-covered banks which rose and fell, and at every village an ancient church amid a garden planted with tombstones.

The train began to slow down. He put his head out of the window and looked along the line. Another station. Windwood, he hoped. It was. He'd arrived. He got out hurriedly, before he could be carried on further; and holding his suitcase in one hand and his typewriter in the other, surveyed the narrow wooden platform.

A porter came lightly up to him and relieved him of his ticket. The train moved off. On one side of the vacant line were cows grazing, on the other a stubble field. He went towards the exit, expecting to find a car waiting for him.

A man in a collarless shirt and torn jacket suddenly appeared. "Are you Mr Pellerin, sir?" he asked. His accent was countrified.

"Yes," said Pellerin, surprised.

"I've coom to take ye to Bezill Tower."

Pellerin felt unable to take his gaze away from the man's ill-fitting teeth. He was very disappointed.

"Gimme ye bag, sir."

And before he knew what was happening, his suitcase and typewriter had been taken out of his hands, and the collarless man was leading him towards the most dilapidated car he had ever seen.

They were placed on the spare seat in the front, and the door to the back of the car was respectfully held open for him.

Pellerin clambered inside. "Does it go?" he asked gloomily, after observing that one of the doors was held in position by string, that the roof sagged, and that the floor was sprinkled with chaff.

"It does!" The owner of the car turned round smiling. "Not always but mostly." And to prove it, he started the engine.

"Well, as long as it gets us there," said Pellerin. "I suppose," he added a moment later in a voice loud enough to be heard above the noise of the engine and the rattling of the loose parts of the bodywork, "Mrs Shakeshaft sent you?"

"She did." He shook his half-turned head as he drove along.

A short silence.

"I've never met her." Pellerin hoped that this remark would bring forth some comment on the lady.

"She rang me oop, and tole me to meet a gentleman this af'noon."

He's not a member of her staff, then, thought Pellerin.

"I sez I couldn't, but she got very angry; so I came along."

Pellerin was surprised. "What about? Does she usually get angry?"

"She's the angriest wooman around these parts," said the driver with disarming brevity.

Pellerin's vision of a refined life at Bezill began to fade, in spite of what Chauncy had said about the food. And yet the salary he was going to be paid was not ungenerous.

Bezill came into sight through a gap in the trees: a large Victorian mansion of blue brick. In one corner was a tall, circular tower. Pellerin wondered what was the origin of the name. Had there been a Bezill? The windows were small, with the exception of one large shallow bay window. He was reminded of an old Dutch fortress, ice-bound, with men skating, the subject of a seventeenth-century oil painting. Ivy grew along the front of the house. It was not lacking in charm of a somewhat gloomy kind.

Mrs Shakeshaft became, in Pellerin's imagination, its tragic prisoner. He must rescue her.

Slender marble pillars of the Doric order were embedded in either side of the front doorway; they served no useful purpose.

The driver stopped, got out, seized Pellerin's luggage and proceeded into the house.

Pellerin followed and found himself in a large hall with a fireplace in the right-hand wall. It was furnished with ugly oak furniture, neither old nor modern, elaborately carved. A hunting horn adorned the chimney-piece, and on a side-table were several square boxes, with glass fronts, containing the masks of foxes.

The driver put down the luggage near the stairs. "They will be 'ere soon," he said, as he passed Pellerin on his way out. "I'll ring the bell."

Pellerin felt disconcerted. He didn't want to be left alone here.

"Good day, sir."

"Good day."

He glanced up at an oil painting of an old man who looked quite startled.

There was the sound of a bell somewhere in the interior.

He turned round as he heard a footstep behind him. A tall, grey-haired man in a morning coat and black striped trousers was approaching. He looked critically at Pellerin; with deferential hostility, Pellerin thought.

"Mr Pellerin?"

"Yes."

"Mrs Shakeshaft is in London. Shall I show you to your room?" He picked up the suitcase but ignored the type-writer, and made off with it up the stairs. Pellerin thought it best to trudge after him.

Damp, he saw, had disfigured the wall-paper, but other-wise the room wasn't bad. A large bed with an ornate brass rail at the head and foot, a water-colour of a young girl with poppies in her hair, a writing-desk. His eye travelled round. A wardrobe, and a bookshelf with several books in it.

The butler had put down his case. He looked at Pellerin.

"May I have your keys, sir?"

The sneer, he thought, had returned. "I never lock my cases," Pellerin replied with elaborate unconcern.

"I will tell Mr Gayfere you are here," said the butler. He began to walk away.

"Who is Mr Gayfere?" asked Pellerin superciliously.

The butler's face registered a flicker of surprise. "Mr Gayfere, sir," he replied with dignity, "lives here."

"Oh, all right," said Pellerin, dismissing him. He glanced away. Had Chauncy, he wondered, ruined the reputation of tutors in the eyes of this butler for all time? Very prob-ably.

As Pellerin came down the stairs, a bald, fat man, was waiting for him.

"Mr Pellerin?" he said. There was warmth in his voice.

"Yes," said Pellerin, still descending. He immediately wished he'd said something a little more momentous.

"How do you do?"

They shook hands on ground-floor level. Gayfere had a lively air.

"Have you been here long?" he asked.

"No, I've just arrived."

A few more pleasantries of this kind.

"Come this way," said Gayfere cheerfully. He set off across the hall.

Pellerin entered the quietness of a library. Here were mahogany bookcases with glazed doors, and arm-chairs round a burning coal fire.

"What will you have to drink?" asked Gayfere.

"A whisky and soda," said Pellerin.

The soda-water rushed out. Gayfere handed Pellerin a tumbler filled with pale yellow liquid and ascending bubbles. Then he poured himself out a glass, taking nearly twice as much whisky.

"What was the journey down like?" Gayfere asked, his blue eyes beneath tufted eyebrows looking searchingly at Pellerin.

"I had rather a long wait at Swanbridge, but having a book to read it didn't matter."

"May I ask what book?"

"Ruskin's *Praeterita*."

"Oh, an excellent work," exclaimed Gayfere.

They talked of Ruskin for a while. Actually, Pellerin had been re-reading on the journey that absurd novel, *Lady Chatterley's Lover*.

Ruskin was dropped for Walter Pater. From Pater to Wilde, at which point Gayfere shuddered and passed hurriedly on to Masefield. He had, apparently, an abhorrence of Wilde.

"And where," said Pellerin, during a pause in this literary conversation, "Is the young man whom I'm to teach? I'm longing to make his acquaintance." He hoped he looked as if he were; he was, in fact, dreading to make his acquaintance. His thoughts on that subject had been mainly dismal.

"Well," said Gayfere, adopting a confidential air, and looking at Pellerin cautiously, "I suppose you'll have to know at some time so you might as well know now." He paused and bent his head slightly towards Pellerin. "He had a fit the other night and . . ."

"A fit?" said Pellerin, interrupting. He was startled. "What sort of fit?"

"You may well ask. Yesterday, his mother took him to see the doctor—a Harley Street specialist—and that was why you were met by Mr Fulalove."

"I see," said Pellerin, glad to learn that there was a reason why he had ridden in that beastly broken-down car, with the springs coming through the leather seat. He relaxed and grew cheerful. There were advantages in teaching a pupil who had fits. He hoped he would have plenty of fits. While the poor boy was doing his best to recover, he would have the time free.

He glanced into his empty glass.

"Have another," said Gayfere. "Help yourself."

After all, thought Pellerin as he poured out the whisky, he does expect me to teach an imbecile.

3

When Pellerin returned to his room, he found his dinner jacket, shirt and black socks laid out. He gazed at them thoughtfully for a moment or two. Where were his cuff links? He hoped he hadn't left them behind. To his relief, he saw them dangling from the cuffs of his white shirt.

It was while lying in the bath that he heard the sound of a gong crashing through the building. He leapt out, seized a towel and began to rub himself vigorously. But Gayfere had distinctly said that dinner was at eight o'clock, he said to himself distressfully. Or could that have been the dressing-gong? He began to relax.

At a quarter to eight, he proceeded downstairs. He found Gayfere in the drawing-room, dressed for dinner, a glass in his hand.

"Good evening, my dear fellow," he said. And with a wave of his hand, "The decanter is over there."

Pellerin poured himself out a glass of sherry.

At eight o'clock precisely, the gong sounded again, to Pellerin's satisfaction. Together they entered the dining-room.

A young man-servant placed a plate of clear soup before him.

"Mrs Shakeshaft rang up. She won't be back till tomorrow," said Gayfere, raising his spoon to his lips.

A silence ensued, during which Pellerin ate his dinner and gazed at the portraits and landscapes on the wall facing him. The landscapes looked as if they had been painted by the men of the portraits, ancestors of the boy he'd come to tutor. From their vacant expressions, Pellerin decided that the disease of his pupil, which he understood to be hereditary, had already set in at the turn of the century.

"Do you know this part of the country at all?" said Gayfere.

"I can't say that I do," replied Pellerin. He paused, then added, "Three years ago I came down here by car for the day to see Gwendoline Barnes." Pellerin did not doubt that Gayfere knew who she was. He felt pleased to be able to claim acquaintance with such a distinguished woman.

Gayfere looked up from his plate. "Gwendoline Barnes?" he said, his face reflecting the effort of trying to remember where he'd heard the name before.

"Her death was reported in *The Times*," said Pellerin helpfully.

"A novelist?"

"No, a Christian." She was, he told Gayfere, the warden of a community of female contemplatives, had written about fifty pamphlets on God, and a lot of poetry.

"Oh, yes, I know who you mean," said Gayfere. "She lived about seven miles from here. I never met her but she was once pointed out to me. She looked as if she was tied up in a sheet," he said disdainfully.

"That was the habit she adopted—she wove the cloth herself, you know," said Pellerin.

"Did she?" said Gayfere. He was wondering why Pellerin had come down to see this crazy old woman. "A relative of yours?" he asked.

"Oh, no."

A pause.

"I wasn't so much interested in her, but in another woman whom she had known in her youth," said Pellerin.

"That must have been a long time ago," said Gayfere. "Wasn't she nearly a hundred when she died?"

"Yes, ninety-eight."

Pellerin began to tell Gayfere of Anna Kingsford, mystic, author of *The Perfect Way*, doctor of medicine, who had died long before he was born, but whom Miss Barnes had known, and about whom he hoped to write a long essay, a book in fact.

Wales, the butler, filled his glass. The young man-servant handed round a dish of vegetables.

"Are you an author, then?" asked Gayfere as he munched away.

"Well," said Pellerin cautiously, "I haven't published anything yet, apart from a few poems here and there."

"Why did you choose her?" said Gayfere. The subject of Pellerin's biography was surely a clue to Pellerin's character, for otherwise he wouldn't have selected this subject. And Gayfere was puzzled about Pellerin's character. His was not an easy face to interpret, and his remarks so far had hardly offered any clues.

"What does he look like?" Mrs Shakeshaft had asked him on the telephone. "Quite presentable," Gayfere had replied. "And serious." "I don't care if he's serious," she had said coolly. "Does he hunt?" "I haven't asked him," Gayfere had replied irritably.

Pellerin could find no reason why he had chosen to write about Anna Kingsford, mystic.

"Do you smoke?" asked Gayfere at the end of dinner.

"Yes, but not often," said Pellerin.

"It's a nasty habit. Give it up. It spoils the palate."

This remark encouraged Pellerin to tell Gayfere that Anna Kingsford had been a vegetarian, as if the eating of meat was a habit as bad as smoking. Moreover, he continued, she was an anti-vivisectionist. In fact, she had studied medicine in order to refute the views of vivisectionists.

In his enthusiasm for the work he was writing, Pellerin

swept on; and Gayfere's expression grew to one of despondency.

"You yourself don't believe in all this, do you?" said Gayfere, unable to contain himself longer.

"Vegetarianism rather appeals to me," said Pellerin, rather taken aback by Gayfere's tone. "I really don't think that all this meat eating is good for one." He glanced down at his lamb cutlet which he'd been eating with relish.

"I think that vegetarianism is a form of madness," said Gayfere, sopping up the gravy on his plate with a piece of bread. "It is like this modern craze which prevents magistrates from sentencing boys to a sound birching."

"Oh?" said Pellerin. He was shocked. "Do you think that corporal punishment is a good thing?"

"A very good thing," said Gayfere. "And not least of all for the boys." He didn't think that Mr Pellerin would be staying with them for long. However, there was something in what he said about anti-vivisectionism. "I'm sure," said Gayfere, "that Mrs Shakeshaft wouldn't like to think of any hound being subjected to this method of pathological research: hounds are sacred to her."

Gayfere had already made up his mind that this Anna Kingsford was one of those wretched women, the first perhaps of a long line since, who expressed absurd sentiments—against birching and about animals. He sincerely hoped that Mr Pellerin, who looked a manly enough fellow, didn't harbour views about the "cruel nature" of blood sports. He was reminded of a local farmer who clasped an exhausted fox to his bosom, preventing the hounds getting at it. "Out of his mind," said Gayfere aloud.

"What?" said Pellerin.

"Did you get what you wanted from that old woman, Gwendoline Barnes?" Gayfere nodded his head in the direction of the window as if she was living next door.

"I'm afraid I didn't. I'd left it too late. She was up and about, but I found, alas, that she was gaga."

"Awful!" exclaimed Gayfere. "These modern drugs keep people alive when they would normally be carried off by pneumonia. Medical science is a mixed blessing."

At the end of the dinner, Gayfere knew rather more about Pellerin. Pellerin had acquired a dimension of depth, was no longer just a name and a face. Pellerin had literary ambitions; he sought out old women for information, and found them gaga (as one always finds them, thought Gayfere sombrely) and he held squeamish views on blood sports—there was no doubt about that, alas. He was, in fact, hovering on the brink of unbelief, and he was not, therefore, the right sort of person to instruct Herbert. Really, the more he thought about it, the worse it seemed. It was absurd not to have asked him before he was engaged what were his views on blood sports. Should he tell Alice about his suspicions? No, what was the good of alarming her? Besides, Herbert did not like blood sports either! (It was excusable in his case for he was an ailing boy, more to be pitied than scolded.) Ah, well, perhaps it wasn't so bad after all. Chauncy had hunted, was an enthusiast for blood sports and a poor tutor—he fornicated with the maid, instead of attending to his duties. No wonder Herbert's Greek was almost nonexistent.

Gayfere ceased thinking on the matter, and turned his attention to the port. It was an imperfect world and growing steadily more imperfect. He wondered if Mr Pellerin was aware that he was drinking a good vintage port.

Nice old stick, thought Pellerin of Gayfere; not so dull as I'd imagined him to be.

4

The library was pleasantly dim. The small Gothic windows had coloured glass in the upper part. Ivy encroached upon them. The walls were lined with books; they climbed above the chimney-piece.

Pellerin extracted one, *Reminiscences of the late Thomas Assheton Smith, Esq. or, the Pursuits of an English Country Gentleman*, dated 1862. He turned the pages. Assheton Smith, Esq. had only one pursuit, and it wasn't women. This was a specialist library of books on fox-hunting, and the histories of great English families who spent most of their lives in the field. The only novels he could discover were by Surtees.

Filled with books, and not one to read, he said to himself. Well, I shan't waste any time here. And time, he thought grimly, was rushing on. He had set himself a dead-line of six months in which to finish writing about Anna Kingsford's visions and dreams, her belief that she had been several notable persons in previous lives. Yes, he had six months with which to do that, and to make up his mind about Gladys. He did not know which was the harder task. Perhaps Mrs Alice Shakeshaft would provide the solution? He was anxiously awaiting her appearance. He began to wonder if anything had happened between her and Chauncy. Something had certainly happened between Chauncy and Beatrice. Where was Beatrice? He imagined her in some attic room, stretched out on the bed, yearning for her lover. He had good news for her! Chauncy was very worried about her. Her eyes would light up when she heard this. But Chauncy had not asked him to give her any message . . .

His thoughts returned to Gladys. The parting from her had not been easy. He had achieved it because he always told her the truth, and she had encouraged him to go. Yes, to go away from her. If she were here now, in this silent library, he would take her in his arms and kiss her tenderly. He had only to tell her of his needs, for her to comply with them. An obliging, friendly girl, Gladys . . .

Gladys! Bring me the moon. He saw her bearing it, like a golden breast, towards him.

The morning post had brought a letter from her. He hadn't opened it yet. It contained, he knew, nothing important. Besides, his thoughts were mainly filled with Mrs Shakeshaft and Beatrice, the St Helenian beauty. But in this sad, silent library, with ivy leaves peeping in through the ancient style windows, he thought of Gladys.

He had kissed her for the first time in the passage of her father's house, in that part of it called the herbarium, the walls of which were lined, not with books on fox-hunting, but with jars, bottles, tins . . . filled with herbs, potions, poisons. Her bald and obese father, Raymond, ran a herbalist's business, mail order only. (He blended his secret remedies, mainly aphrodisiacs and long-life potions, and posted them overseas to foreign gentlemen who wanted to bolster up their virility, and who feared death. His desk was always littered with letters bearing gorgeous foreign stamps).

"What is that?" he had asked her, pressing his cheek against hers, and looking over her shoulder at one particular jar. It bore a label, and on it was printed GENUINE DAMIANA LEAVES. He had read this out aloud.

"Oh, please don't," she had said, moving in his arms. Her cheek had grown warm. Remorselessly, he had continued reading the label. "This somewhat scarce herb is sold solely by us for its high tonic potency to the genital organs of both sexes."

"Oh, you are mean!"

She had torn herself free and fled.

She was a prude, really—a prude in a herbarium.

None of the leaves or potions in Mr Raymond Pasquier's herbarium had helped his wife to conceive, and jars of his Elixir of Life powders "a remarkable plant from the East") had failed to save her from dying at the age of fifty-one. But meanwhile they had adopted Gladys,—green-eyed, snub-nosed Gladys, now assistant in the herbarium. Her job was to do up and address the packages, and take them to the post.

In the morning, Gayfere took Pellerin through several rooms on the ground floor, led him into the music-room. It was as big as a barn, and open to the roof. In a large bay window was a grand piano. Gayfere pointed to the carpet, told him that it had been made according to a design drawn especially by William Morris, "It has been in this room ever since."

"How interesting," said Pellerin, but his gaze had already shifted from the floral pattern of the carpet to the window, through which he could see the back view of a young woman with broad hips, stretching up to hang a tea-cloth on a line. Now she had turned round. Her skin was as dark as olive, her eyes light-coloured, her hair jet black. She reminded Pellerin of a photograph he had seen of a black jaguar.

"Fascinating," he said, glancing back to the carpet.

"Yes, it is, isn't it?" said Gayfere, moving on.

"Very," said Pellerin. What hips! He thought of Chauncy, and sighed. The whole matter was clear now.

He asked Gayfere to show him the tower, but this Gayfere declined to do—because of the stairs. He couldn't climb stairs, he said. Pellerin was surprised. He had seen Gayfere mount the staircase in the hall without any effort at all.

Before dinner, Pellerin went out for a walk, found the village and *The Leg and Seven Stars*, glad name for a pub.

As he entered, "the oldest inhabitant," who was sitting on a bench against the panelled wall, glanced up at him keenly. Above the chimney-piece was a fish in a glass case. Its shiny back gleamed in the dim light. A large pike, captured by one Walter Crewkerne in the summer of 1911. Pellerin read this on a brass tablet screwed on the frame.

"Good evening, sir," said the barman.

Pellerin asked for cider, local cider.

The face of the pike reminded him of Raymond Pasquier: its eye was the same colour as his eye, and they shared the same sharp expression.

This train of thought led to the still unopened letter in his pocket. He'd forgotten about it. Without enthusiasm, he took it out and laid it on the polished oak table, beside his pint of cider. *Geoffrey Pellerin Esq.* and the address, in small neat handwriting, but with little ambitious flourishes above, and large loops of misery below.

He picked up his glass of cider and held it momentarily in the air in line with the pike, as if to drink the health of Mr Pasquier—the pike, alas, had no health to consider any more, but by its size it seemed to have lived successfully and even for a considerable time until the fatal day . . .

The cider was cloudy. The real stuff, thought Pellerin. He drew the glass to his lips, and drank. When he set it down, the level had receded by an inch. He leant back and glanced at the pike again; then with a sigh, he opened Gladys's letter which had been lying in his pocket for a couple of days— forgotten, neglected, due to the excitement of coming to Windwood and taking up the post of resident tutor to a boy who had fits.

(In his mind's eye, he saw the boy, no longer having fits, no longer having anything, but lying still at last, and embalmed in a glass coffin alongside the terror of the stream in this bar.)

It was not a long letter.

Darling Geoffrey,

Well, good luck. I hope you will like the boy. And the boy's mother, and the boy's father. I'm dying to know all.

If she knew, thought Pellerin, that the boy has no father, she'd give me up for lost.

And I hope you will have a comfortable bed!

Yes, his bed was quite comfortable, and while he was in it this morning, the house-boy had brought him a cup of tea.

"Good morning, sir," he'd said. "It's half past eight."

His voice was like the voice of Mr Fulalove, who'd driven him to Bezill Tower, a country brogue.

Daddy is mystified why you decided to go off. I said it was on impulse—isn't that right?

Yes, that's right. I didn't want to get caught like that pike. His glance travelled towards the pike. Mr Crewkerne must have had a fright when he pulled you out of the river.

He said tutoring wasn't your line at all, and I replied: What does it matter? You're not going to do it for long.

What was his line? He wished he knew. Beatrice perhaps. Raymond Pasquier had offered to teach him the secrets of the alchemists' art. A tempting bait. She would make a good wife. She looked, with her snub nose, the sort of woman who would be that.

"But he must be a quack," his father had said. "No honest man would sell aphrodisiacs."

"I don't see why," he'd argued, not liking his father's cocksure attitude. (His father was a lawyer.)

"Why are you so interested in Mr Pasquier?" his mother had asked.

"I'm not," he'd replied. He didn't want to tell her about Gladys.

Pellerin drank up his cider. It was heady stuff, of the genuine apple and without any cunning additions to give it a brassy hue. One could easily get drunk on it.

Yes, he was unhappy about Gladys because, simply, she expected him to marry her. He could see one reason for doing this: it would solve her problem. But would it solve his? He doubted it.

"Good night," he said to the oldest inhabitant as he made his way past him to the door. The barman had vanished.

The oldest inhabitant did not reply, as if he had not heard or understood what Pellerin had said.

He began to walk back to Bezill. It came in sight in the moonlight, the tower round and stout. Why hadn't Gayfere taken him up there?

A powerful car stood in the drive before the front door, a Humber Snipe. Mrs Shakeshaft and boy had arrived back.

As he entered the dimly-lit, empty hall, he was assailed by a feeling of loneliness, of isolation from everyone he knew and loved. He took off his coat and, as he stretched out his hand to hang it up on an iron peg (one of several in a row), he caught sight of a child's coat, a boy's, a small boy's. It wasn't there when he had gone out. But surely his pupil was bigger than that?

While he was turning these thoughts over in his mind, the light at the top of the stairs was switched on. A moment later the head and shoulders of a little man appeared above the balustrade. A manikin, thought Pellerin. How odd. Now he was at the stairhead. Mrs Shakeshaft's dwarf brother, perhaps. He had a large head, surrounded by a mop of hair, and a sad and sallow face of indeterminate age.

With a start, Pellerin realized that this was Herbert whom he'd come to teach.

He was standing there, hesitating.

He is too embarrassed to come down, thought Pellerin. He went to the foot of the stairs.

"Hallo," he said, looking up.

The manikin ceased gazing at his feet, and looked down at Pellerin.

"Hallo," he said, in an alto voice. He began to descend.

He was a small boy; he did not look twelve, let alone fifteen which was his age—or so Pellerin had been told.

"Are you Herbert?" Pellerin said when he drew level.

"Yes," said the boy.

Pellerin felt like laughing. Had he come here to teach this creature Greek? Oh, this was impossible!

"I'm Mr Pellerin," he said, introducing himself. "I'm your new tutor."

There were dark shadows under his eyes as if he hardly slept, but the eyes themselves were large and china blue. With his mop of hair, he looked like an insipid version of Swinburne. This notion prompted Pellerin to ask him—he was searching for something to say: "Do you write poetry, Herbert?"

For a moment the sallowness departed from Herbert's face, and a look of pleasure shone in his azure eyes.

"Yes," he said. "How did you know?"

"You look like a poet," Pellerin said. He did think that there was something "poetical" about Herbert, something in his face remote and full of longing.

"Oh," said the boy. For him to have been told that he looked like a poet was equivalent to saying that he was a poet, and to be a poet, at his age, was to be among the gods.

This is a good beginning, thought Pellerin.

Suddenly a loud jarring noise rang out. Pellerin glanced in the direction it came from, and saw Wales, in the distant corner of the hall, putting back in its place the instrument with which he had beaten the gong.

5

Mrs Shakeshaft apologised for not being at home to receive
him; then she broke the good news. For the next three
months at least, Herbert was to have only an hour's lesson
in the morning and another in the afternoon, instead of
two hours in the morning and another two after lunch.
The delicate state of his health made more work than this
inadvisable.

Pellerin saw his work cut down by half. Things looked
bright indeed for his book on Anna Kingsford. As for prepa-
ration, Herbert should do only as much as he felt inclined to
do. His brain must not be overloaded.

I certainly won't do that, said Pellerin to himself. He
decided that Herbert needed plenty of sympathy, more
sympathy than instruction. He wondered what had brought
him to this sorry impasse, so that the poor boy could only
protest by throwing a fit—or that, at least, was the way
in which he saw it. What a good thing I've come to Bezill
Tower, thought Pellerin. And he began to look forward to
many a pleasant hour with Herbert in field and lane, talking
of flowers and poetry.

When Pellerin had caught sight of Mrs Shakeshaft, all
his romantic notions about her evaporated. He had met the
reality, an edge of it at least. She was in her thirties, had a
quite handsome but entirely sexless face, and with none of
the anger reflected in it that he had been led to expect. There
was a distinct firmness about the jaw. She was, he realized
disappointedly, cold—a cold, proud, stubborn woman,

not a woman with whom it would be wise to disagree. He began to feel more sorry for her than for Herbert, whom he could see properly for the first time—he was sitting at the other end of the table opposite to his mother at the table head. He really was an odd-looking sensitive creature.

Herbert said nothing. It was Gayfere who did most of the talking. And Mrs Shakeshaft listened, engrossed; or perhaps she only appeared to be out of politeness.

She behaves, Pellerin thought, as if she is in love with him, a notion which struck him as strange until he recollected that he had heard, or read in some book, that women sometimes fall in love with frightful men—frightful to others, that is.

Gayfere was scornful: "His talk was repeated twice; three broadcasts and all because he'd had lunch with Max Beerbohm on one occasion. I had lunch with him a hundred times. I stayed for several months with him in his villa at Rapallo—not much of a place. He was there for forty years and never learnt Italian—but his Italian neighbours liked him, he was popular."

"Did you hear what kind of day they had?" asked Mrs Shakeshaft.

"Oh, wonderful! A nine mile point and killed in the open," replied Gayfere.

An expression of pain passed over Herbert's face. It was the fox which had been killed in the open. He looked down into his plate as Gayfere began to tell Mrs Shakeshaft the details—a friend, whom Gayfere had met that morning in the village, had told him.

Pellerin's and Herbert's eyes met: it seemed to Pellerin that Herbert was begging him not to approve of this killing of the fox, of this whole business of hunting.

Pellerin shrugged his shoulders slightly and glanced away. He knew nothing about the subject; he couldn't quite imagine himself in pursuit of the fox, but . . . It really was an issue he was incapable of judging. He thought of Chauncy's remark about being mounted once a fortnight. Of course, if Herbert would rather he didn't take any part in it . . .

"Were you brought up in a hunting country?" The question, Pellerin realized, was being addressed to him.

"Yes, but my father disapproved of it."

As a matter of fact, his father hadn't any views on the matter. They were not grand enough to hunt.

Mrs Shakeshaft made no comment, but her face seemed to recede, disappointedly, from him. He caught Herbert's eye. Herbert glanced away, but his face, Pellerin saw, was flushed with pleasure.

"It takes all sorts to make a world," said Gayfere, feeling he should say something.

The subject was dropped, and soon they were talking about the teaching of Greek today.

Looking very serious, Pellerin told Mrs Shakeshaft that until Herbert was ready to absorb more than an hour's Greek a day, he would not make rapid progress. (He felt he should make some reference to his duties, and protect himself from the accusation, which might later be levelled at him, that he had taught the boy nothing. Yes, the outlook for Anna Kingsford, mystic and vegetarian, was bright indeed.)

"He mustn't be overworked," said Mrs Shakeshaft, talking as if Herbert was not there at the table, "but do please take him to all the meets, and there is no reason why he shouldn't follow a little way on foot, and see the first draw."

She had spoken so keenly that Pellerin felt that she was more interested in her son's physical health than in the cultivation of his mind. He was going to reply, "But does he need all this exercise?" when he realized that he'd misunderstood her.

"Oh, certainly," he said. They could soon lose track of the hunt, he thought. He glanced searchingly into her pale eyes: was she interested only in hunting? Didn't anything else exist for her?

They all stood up.

"I'll leave you to your port," said Mrs Shakeshaft, and with a smile for Pellerin, she left the room.

"Good night," said Herbert. His face softened as he looked at his tutor and bowed slightly to him. He followed his mother, closing the door behind him.

Pellerin was invited to move into Mrs Shakeshaft's place, so that he was diagonal to Gayfere.

"Fonseca '48," said Gayfere, tapping the decanter.

As he sipped his port, Gayfere said, "It's a great pity you don't hunt. I myself am prevented for medical reasons." He did not enlarge on this.

Soon they were talking about literature, a subject equally dear to Gayfere's heart. He told Pellerin that, as a young man, his whole outlook had been changed by reading André Gide's *Les Nourritures Terrestres*. He had written to Gide and thanked him from the bottom of his heart for the sentiments on life and art that are expressed in that work.

And a year later, at Taormina, he met the great man himself. At the sight of him, he was overcome with emotion.

Gayfere had not been alone, but in the company of a fellow undergraduate who was to distinguish himself as a designer of racing cars. The occasion was a lively, not to say a joyous, one, and it was marred only by its abrupt termination the following morning when Gide had found these two young men in bed together: there was a third person between them, hidden beneath the bedclothes, a person who turned out to be—to Gide's surprise and disappointment—a young woman.

Gayfere described the incident as if it had no connection whatsoever with Gide's sudden loss of interest in the two young Englishmen. Gayfere had failed to grasp the point.

But how was this possible in view of Gide's frank confessions? Was Gayfere assuming an attitude of innocence? Surely he realized at the time—or learnt later—that Gide had thought they were young men of a certain type, a type common enough, whom Karl Heinrich Ulrichs called Urnings? Pellerin wondered if Gayfere had ever heard of this word. Perhaps the subject was so abhorrent to him that he suppressed involuntarily any knowledge of it, and like those three monkeys neither saw, heard nor spoke any such evil. Is it, Pellerin asked himself, sheer naiveté which makes a man behave so innocently? Or had fear descended like a hatchet upon his mind and split off several fragments, so that he could deny and ignore what everyone else accepted? And where had it led him? And what was it doing to him? Pellerin doubted if he would ever find out, but he thought it all fascinating. Yes, fascinating.

"You should write your memoirs," he said lazily, gazing benevolently at the florid face before him.

"I am writing them," promptly replied Gayfere. He mentioned a firm of publishers who were waiting impatiently for the typescript, but "They will just have to wait. I'm not a journalist who can dash things off."

At ten o'clock Pellerin went upstairs to bed. The port had given him a feeling of lightness and contentment: the future, it seemed, stretched out pleasantly before him. Really, it was a fortunate thing to have come to Bezill; and if Mrs Shakeshaft had proved disappointing, there was always Beatrice. Perhaps it was an understood thing in this household that the resident tutor slept with the foreign maid. She was probably paid a little extra for this duty.

With these thoughts in his mind, he opened the bedroom door: there was no need to grope for the light switch for there was a light already in the room. It came, to his surprise, from a night-light burning in a saucer. In a small low bed was a youth with a mop of hair. His face was oddly familiar. The large eyes of the boy stared at him without alarm.

He had entered Herbert's bedroom by mistake. With a muttered apology, he began to withdraw, but Herbert called out, "Don't go."

"Did I wake you up?"

"No, I wasn't asleep."

"I can't find my room," Pellerin said.

"It's opposite mine."

Herbert propped himself up on his elbow, and looked with curiosity as well as with respect at his tutor. For a while neither spoke. Why has he a night-light? thought Pellerin. He couldn't withdraw without a few more words. Suddenly, he made a surprising discovery. Herbert was quite good-looking in bed, for then one didn't know how short he was, and the yellowish night-light concealed instead of revealed the yellowish pallor of his face.

"A little Greek in the morning," Pellerin said, light-heartedly. "By the way, do you know any?"

"Not really; the alphabet, and even that I don't know as well as I should."

"What's the difficulty?"

"There are three letters I keep on mixing up: the *psi* and the *chi* and the other one that I can hardly pronounce."

Pellerin made a mixed guttural and hissing sound for the letter which in English is represented by *xi*. "Yes, that's a difficult one."

Downstairs, Mrs Shakeshaft was saying to Gayfere, "It never occurred to me to ask him if he hunted. I took it for granted." She paused, and then added with a sigh, "Well, there's nothing we can do about it now. He probably won't stay with us for long. Next time we must be more careful."

6

It seemed that Gayfere had known many celebrated literary men, such as D. H. Lawrence and Norman Douglas, who had died some time since. And between the wars he had made the acquaintance of many a person whose name appears in the *Almanack de Gotha*: he had been wandering backwards and forwards across the continent of Europe, from Schloss to château, as the guest of this or that noble person until, on the death of Captain Shakeshaft, he had been offered a permanent home at Bezill. It was as good a place as any in which to write his memoirs.

"Tell me, how long has Mr Gayfere been here?"

Pellerin suddenly threw this question at Herbert in the course of a discussion on the third declension of Greek nouns.

"Oh, ages," said Herbert, relieved to change the subject. "He's always been here, as long as I remember."

"Your father knew him?"

"Yes," said Herbert.

He went on to tell Pellerin of a quarrel which had taken place when he was about four years of age. He remembered some details. His father had asked Gayfere to leave the house. "But my mother in a terrible rage shouted something and my father left instead. The next thing I heard was that he was dead."

Pellerin was at a loss for words. He grew embarrassed when he saw the glint of tears in Herbert's eyes.

"I hate Gayfere," said Herbert.

"Do you?" said Pellerin, wondering what he should say

to this. He decided to be simply frank. "I'm not surprised," he said.

Herbert gave him a glance of gratitude.

"Let's get on with the lesson, shall we?" said Pellerin softly. He waited a moment or two until Herbert had gathered his thoughts together. "Now, there are two main groups in the third declension: those nouns with consonant stems and those with vowel stems . . ."

Two days later, he met Herbert by chance amid the trees on the edge of the park. He was accompanied by his brown spaniel, Charlie. They walked along together.

"I saw an ant yesterday," said Herbert. "I suppose the sunshine brought it out." He told his tutor that only a warm November day—it was now November—will bring out an ant.

They stopped before a cluster of flat white stones with shaped tops. They were inscribed.

Wonk aged 14, read Pellerin, and the date beneath, 1889. The name of *Ginger* was on another of these small tombstones, and *Sambo* on a third.

"The pets' cemetery," said Herbert.

The earliest date was 1873.

The occasion reminded Herbert of a grave in another place; for he produced from his trouser pocket a little wallet, extracted a photograph from it, and gave it to Pellerin. It was of a youngish man in the full-dress uniform of the Blues. "My father," he said.

Pellerin scrutinized the face of Captain Shakeshaft.

"You look like him," he said, as he handed the photograph back. It was a remark which brought a flush of pleasure to Herbert's face.

"Do you know," said Herbert, changing the subject, "that Charlie never cocks his leg in this spot."

Charlie at that moment was gazing reverently at one of the tombstones.

7

Pellerin's imagination was largely preoccupied by three women. There was Gladys, who wrote to him once or twice a week from London; Beatrice, whom he would sometimes see at eight o'clock in the morning entering Mrs Shakeshaft's bedroom with a tray in her hands; and Mrs Shakeshaft, his employer.

He wrote Gladys light-hearted, restrained letters in reply to hers, telling her about his life at Windwood, of the progress of his work on Anna Kingsford—he regularly received through the post books from the London Library—of his growing sense of hopelessness (at his advanced age of twenty-three) . . . He wanted her to realize that, in spite of his knowledge of the classics, modern languages, and his possession of a second-class degree, he was unworthy of taking over her father's herbarium and of making a fortune out of aphrodisiacs. To which Gladys replied, *Darling, don't be silly* . . .

He thought of Gladys least of all.

Beatrice, a girl with magnificent hips. He was not surprised that Chauncy had left in disgrace because of her. Why hadn't she been given the sack too? Banishment to St Helena, he supposed, was too severe a punishment, reserved only for major criminals. And what had she done?

Pellerin turned these thoughts over in his mind, especially at night before falling asleep. Had she gone to Chauncy's bedroom, or he to hers? Perhaps in this very room, on this actual bed . . . And were they caught *in flagrante*? He stretched himself restlessly, tried to fall asleep while lying on his other side.

At week-ends, when there was usually a party of guests, Beatrice would help at the dining-table. And whenever Pellerin's glance met hers, she would cast her eyes down. Does she expect me, Pellerin wondered, to fill the vacancy left by Chauncy? He found the notion fascinating, and was reminded of a passage in *The Republic*.

> *And is there any pleasure you can name that is greater and keener than sexual pleasure?*
> *No; nor any that is more like frenzy.*

Plato had it all.

At nine, Mrs Shakeshaft would descend to breakfast, wearing white breeches and an elaborate stock. She also wore at this hour a white apron to protect her white breeches. The first time Pellerin saw this white apron, it was draped round one of the male guests. He looked at it with discreet surprise. He was astonished when Mrs Shakeshaft appeared in a similar apron. A week or so later, when he'd grown accustomed to the sight of this attire, she explained:

"I'm thought rather an eccentric round here, but I couldn't see why the men should go out with clean breeches and I shouldn't."

In jack-boots, equipped with flask and sandwich case, she would step into her car and be driven away to the meet, her groom, with two horses, having ridden on ahead.

Pellerin liked to see her depart. She looked, he thought, rather defenceless in black coat and white stock, and a little sad.

She hunted at least four days a week. "When you have horses, you have to take them out," she said to him when the subject arose in conversation: she considered that he ought to know this.

8

Mrs Shakeshaft, Pellerin decided, was terrified of death. She was obviously terrified of something: her coldness towards her only child; the suicide of her husband; Gayfere, her companion—this all pointed to some complex or other, some terrible fear which was probably deeply buried in her subconscious, but was all the more potent for that.

Pellerin's expression was stern and deeply thoughtful as he turned these notions over in his mind. Yes, death. Perhaps her passion for hunting was only an attempt, symbolically speaking, to ride away from the ultimate enemy. She always returned to the house, mud-spattered, exhausted, ravenously hungry.

As she came in at dusk one evening, Wales, who was waiting for her, said:

"I am sorry to tell you, madam, but the telegram people rang up and gave me this message." He handed her the text of the message, but she declined it with a wave of her crop, exclaiming, "Oh, just tell me!"

Wales, who knew the message off by heart, put on his glasses and read out as if for the first time, and in his most solemn manner: "Regret to inform you that Sir Roger Noakes died peacefully this morning." He paused, and then added, "It is signed Vavasor."

Without any comment, Mrs Shakeshaft proceeded on her way.

Sir Roger was her father.

It was the sequel a few days later which led Pellerin to the view that she had a horror of death.

She had appeared as usual in riding breeches and white apron.

Gayfere, who was eating his breakfast, looked at her in surprise.

"But it's the funeral today. Aren't you going?"

"Quite impossible. I'm hunting today. I never miss the Tuesday country if I can possibly help it."

At that moment Pellerin was helping himself to coffee at the sideboard.

Gayfere opened his mouth to reply, but thought better of it and fell silent.

Wales was summoned, and ordered to ring up a florist and have a very nice wreath despatched post haste. Mrs Shakeshaft emphasized that it was to be a very nice wreath; no ordinary one, in fact.

9

"What is the view like from the tower?" asked Pellerin.

"Oh, it's a wonderful view: one can see the sea on a clear day," replied Herbert.

"Is it clear enough today?" said Pellerin, glancing through the window. He was keen to go up the tower and survey the countryside. "The sun's shining," he said, and went close to the window, and looked out at a blue sky decorated with only a few late clouds. "What a splendid day for hunting," he said drily.

He found Herbert looking a little embarrassed. "I shall have to ask Mother's permission to take you up there."

"Oh?"

"You see, it's locked, and she has the key. I'm not allowed to go up there."

"Is she afraid you'll tumble off?"

"No, it's not that . . ."

Pellerin looked sharply at him as he fell silent.

"She'll refuse, of course," Herbert said. He looked thoughtfully at his tutor. "I've got a key. But no one knows that." He added with bravado: "I sometimes go up there."

He looked apprehensively at Pellerin who was wondering what secrets the tower contained. The view no longer interested him.

"What is up there?" he asked. Why had Gayfere declined to take him up?

"My father's things," said Herbert, "and my aunt's."

"Your aunt's?"

"Yes, Aunt Marion. She's locked up, you know, in the looney bin."

"Is she, now?" said Pellerin. "For keeps?"

"I'm afraid so," said Herbert with a sigh—a genuine sigh.

"Never let out?"

"Oh, never. She screams sometimes, I gather."

"Have you heard her scream?"

Herbert shook his head. No, he hadn't actually heard her screams ring out from a window high up in the looney bin, but that was what he'd thought he'd been told or overheard, unless of course it was in his wilder dreams.

"Where is the looney bin?"

"Up north."

They were down south, and in sight of the sea on clear days from the top of the tower which was always kept locked.

"Miles away, eh?"

"Oh, miles."

"Out of sight as well as out of mind," said Pellerin. He grinned at Herbert. A good pun, that.

"Oh, very much out of mind," said Herbert, laughing. Suddenly he covered his mouth with his hand, grew sad. Then he said, "I love Aunt Marion, and I'm not allowed to see her. I believe I could make her sane, if I talked to her, but I'm not allowed to. My mother said, 'Oh, don't be absurd,' when I suggested it. I once wrote to her, but didn't know her address, so I asked my mother and she said she'd address the letter and post it for me, but I never got a reply. Perhaps Aunt Marion can't spell any more, having lost her wits, I mean."

"And all her spelling has fallen out and been lost," said Pellerin, thinking that not unlikely. The daft can't spell. And yet even an ill-spelt letter is better than none. He wondered what had been the relationship between Aunt Marion and Captain Shakeshaft. And because his mind ran along amorous lines, he began to think of them as lovers. Yes, they had been lovers, a sinful affair, driving the one to death and the other to despair and madness. There was a mystery behind the locked door which guarded the tower. And Herbert had a duplicate key under a floor board or inside the throat of one of the stuffed birds in his room, innocent in its glass case—ivory towers within ivory towers, worlds within worlds.

"You don't think the letter was posted, do you?"

Herbert looked at his tutor in an empty, abstracted way for a moment or two before replying; then he said, with a little disarming laugh, "I don't think it was."

"*I* certainly don't think so," said Pellerin. "I wonder what your mother did with it?"

"Burnt it."

"You don't think she framed it and hung it up somewhere?"

Herbert thought this a fine joke, although at his expense. "I concluded the letter," he said, "with the words *With love from Herbert*." The idea seized his imagination, and he saw his letter framed and hung up in some secret place, madhouse or dovecote, with these words, fading fast, clearly shown: *With love from Herbert*. Yes, from Herbert. Let the pigeons take the message to her, and defeat his mother's design. "My love for Aunt Marion," he said. "But where?" There was an expression of pain on his sad, sallow face.

"Where?" said Pellerin, wondering what he meant.

"Where hung up? In the tower? I haven't seen it there. No, no!"

"Will you take me up to look?"

"Of course, of course!" said Herbert fervently.

Their friendship, their real friendship could be traced back to this moment, Pellerin thought.

"Herbert," he said.

"Yes."

"Is your aunt your mother's or your father's sister?" His whole theory hung on Herbert's reply.

"My mother's."

"Ah," said Pellerin. He waited a moment or two before putting his next question. "What did your father think of Aunt Marion?"

Herbert shrugged his shoulders: that was something he simply did not know. "I don't think they saw much of each other," he said.

A good thing he hasn't a suspicious mind, thought Pellerin. Or is it merely experience he lacks? He doesn't know. After all, his father died when he was four.

"But it's a funny thing," continued Herbert, "both my aunt's and my father's things are up in the tower, in the same room, all mixed up, flung down, coats and hats and books muddled together. Or, rather, they were, but I've tidied them up a bit, sorted out the books, his and hers, and hung up the clothes. I thought burglars had been there. You know the sort of thing they do, pull out drawers and leave everything in a frightful mess. But I now think it was my mother, she's my aunt's next-of-kin, and took charge of all her things when she was locked up in the looney bin. She never goes up there, so she doesn't know I've tidied everything up, shaken the dust out of them."

"Shall we go up and see?" said Pellerin impatiently.

"Do you want to see the view?"

"Yes," said Pellerin, but the view from the top no longer interested him, at least, not in the sense which Herbert meant.

"It's a jolly good view."

"Do you watch birds from there?"

"In the winter, I've leant out of the window and chucked

pieces of bread at the gulls. They always swoop down and catch them before they can reach the ground. It's jolly good sport, but they made such a noise that Gayfere was woken up and he came out to look. I just managed to dart back in time. 'The gulls are attacking the tower,' he said at dinner. My mother looked at me suspiciously."

"It's a kind of lumber-room up there, I take it?" said Pellerin, thinking of letters and diaries, not of views, gulls and pieces of bread hurled about.

"Yes, everything has been dragged up there—some pretty things. Aunt Marion's 'cello. They might have let her take her 'cello—a valuable one, I'm told—to the looney bin with her, but my mother decreed that she shouldn't, although she begged for it, and even cried."

"Oh, god, didn't they let her take her 'cello?" said Pellerin. "Why not?" The thought upset him.

"Because it would annoy the other lunatics," said Herbert simply. "And they would jump in it, hit her on the head with it, throw it through the window."

"Do you believe that?"

"No, I don't. On the contrary, I think her playing would charm them, perhaps cure them. Who knows?"

Even if she played atrociously, thought Pellerin. Anyhow, it wouldn't drive them mad—they're that already.

10

After lunch, Herbert said, "While Gayfere sleeps ..." And he drew from his pocket a long shining key.

Pellerin said nothing, but followed his fellow conspirator upstairs.

Herbert made a detour to his room, returned quickly with a pair of binoculars.

"Good idea," said Pellerin.

"We may catch a glimpse of the hunt. With these I might even pick out my mother, see how she's going."

"I hope she won't see us."

"No," said Herbert thoughtfully. His mother would be keeping a sharp look out for the fox, her gaze was not tower-wards, but down to earth.

They ascended a narrow staircase, which Pellerin had not noticed before, to the second floor of the house.

"No one ever comes up here," said Herbert, "except me, and I don't come up here often."

He climbs secretly into the tower, thought Pellerin, to brood and daydream. A long gallery hung with paintings met his gaze. He stopped to look at a small seascape by an early 19th century English painter. The artist's name was not painted on the frame. He looked for a signature, but there wasn't one which he could see. He thought it might be by Bonington. The next painting was obviously by George Morland.

"I say, these are good," he said.

"They were my great-grandfather's," said Herbert. "He collected pictures. Some of them have been illustrated in books and magazines, but my mother couldn't care less. She's only interested in hunting. If they were of famous horses or hunting scenes, that would be different—she'd tolerate them then."

"But you've got masterpieces here," said Pellerin. His gaze ran along the wall. "This is a Constable," he said, pointing to the picture in front of him. He looked at it in admiration and surprise; then he glanced avidly at the next painting and moved on. "Hallo, this looks like a Delacroix." He went close. "It is." He turned round to look at Herbert. "Your great-grandfather collected fashionable pictures," he said drily. Most of them were still in fashion.

"I didn't know that you were interested in paintings," said Herbert.

"I'm interested in everything," said Pellerin. The image of Mrs Shakeshaft came to his mind. Was he interested in her? What on earth for? She was cold, she was not attractive sexually (at least to him), her mind was filled with things that he was completely unrelated to. The image crystallised into a woman (looking not unlike Mrs Shakeshaft) in a black coat, mounted, crop in hand, a firmness about her chin, her golden hair showing in a small bun beneath her bowler hat.

"We sometimes get letters from chaps inquiring about a painting. We've got one by William Blake of Satan, you know. Mother always gets Gayfere to write back and say, 'Sorry, burnt.' Destroyed in the fire of '28. There was a fire then, I think, but it didn't burn much."

"That's a good way out."

"I sometimes think that mother really wishes they were burnt, the lot of them. She's only interested in—well, not in art. And she doesn't want chaps coming round to look at grandfather's paintings, pestering her to sell them or lend them to this or that exhibition. 'Blow art,' she says."

"What a woman!" ejaculated Pellerin.

Suddenly he saw Gayfere's head and shoulders appear at the top of the stairs, and stay there, just the head and shoulders as if his feet had got stuck.

"What are you doing here?" he said in an unfriendly voice. The question was addressed to Herbert.

There was an awkward silence. Herbert was too abashed to say anything, and Pellerin was rather at a loss for words.

"I'm just showing Mr Pellerin round," said Herbert at last.

"I've shown him round already," said Gayfere. Then he added in a more normal voice, and even with a touch of kindness, "Do come down." And he began to disappear beneath the floor level, like Punch.

Pellerin returned his attention to the Delacroix. It was of someone cutting off someone else's head. He thought it was Gayfere's head which was being cut off.

For two or three minutes neither of them spoke or moved. Herbert was deep in thought. Then he went to the stairhead and looked down. He turned round to Pellerin. "He's gone," he said. He came over to his tutor. "I thought he was asleep at this time." He added after a pause, "Shall we continue?"

"I'd rather not," said Pellerin. "Not today, anyhow."

"He won't come up again."

"You never know." Pellerin gazed thoughtfully at his pupil. "Nice chap, Gayfere," he said.

"I hate him," said Herbert. His china blue eyes met Pellerin's frankly. He was not ashamed of his hatred of Gayfere.

"What did your father think of Gayfere? Or perhaps you don't remember?"

"Oh, I do. He hated him. He just hated him." Herbert spoke with deep satisfaction.

"Is that why you hate him?" asked Pellerin.

Herbert found the question disconcerting; he looked thoughtfully at Pellerin and did not answer.

"And your father's things are up there?" said Pellerin, pointing ceilingwards, changing the subject.

"Yes, the lot. Mother can't bear anything that reminds her of him."

"Except you," said Pellerin.

"Oh," said Herbert, surprised. "Do you think she likes me?"

"Of course," replied Pellerin as if the contrary was impossible, absurd even.

"I don't think she does," said Herbert simply. "I don't hunt."

Pellerin decided that Mrs Shakeshaft was as cold as an ice lolly or as cold—he searched for a suitable simile—as the stone floor of a church in winter. Yes, that was pretty cool. It was not surprising that he found her conversation dull. It seemed to him that she never spoke her mind or ever said anything that wasn't utterly conventional. And yet she did wear a white apron for breakfast, so as not to soil her beautiful clean breeches, and that was as odd as it was sensible. She couldn't, he reasoned, be all that conventional and dull. And he personally didn't of course find her dull. A woman one is in love with is never dull. What, then, was wrong with her? There was certainly something wrong with her. She didn't, Pellerin decided, live from her own centre—that was what was wrong with her. But where was her centre, and how did he know that she was living off-centre? Because she took no notice of him? Off-centre, off-beat. She didn't like him! But why didn't she like him? Because he didn't hunt? No, it was deeper than that. It was, simply, she was unaware of his existence.

She was about thirty-five—too young to resign herself to boredom, and the company of Percy Gayfere.

"What a waste of a good woman," he said to himself, as he wandered disconsolate through the wood.

12

He liked Herbert. The boy had a sweet nature. He was keen and intelligent; he was easy to teach. In six weeks a warm friendship had sprung up between them. They would go for walks together, talking of nature—flowers, birds, worms and their habits.

Herbert wrote nature poems. Some of them he showed Pellerin. They were in iambic metre. He also wrote other poems. The thoughts of a schoolboy in verse form. Pellerin detected something in them which was striving to break out from the restraints of conventional thought, and conventional form. And some of his poems were less conventional in form. The one, for instance, that began:

> The cry of the cuckoo in the night
> Cuckoo cuckoo!
> Disturbs my sad dream . . .

Was this poem, Pellerin wondered, based upon a real experience? Had he actually been awakened from a dream, a sad dream, by the cuckoo in the night? He must ask him.

How different the boy was from his mother! She repressed her feelings, was as cold as an ice lolly; he tried to express his. He made up for her. Wasn't it time he wrote a few love poems? To the Sweet Lady of my Dreams. The omissions of the one generation are made up for by the next. Would Herbert, in the fulness of time, become a regular Casanova? No, Pellerin couldn't imagine him pursuing women with ferocious intent. He was too sensitive, too kind for that.

He quite liked Gayfere. Gayfere was, at least, someone to talk to; he was not as cold as an ice lolly. One had, at first, to overcome one's disgust of him . . . Pellerin was thinking of his bloated appearance.

Herbert went to bed early.

There was television in the library, and Anna Kingsford waited for him in his room.

As for Mrs Shakeshaft, he was at a loss to know what to say to her: she had become a superior kind of being, whose conversation about fox-hunting was almost beyond his understanding.

Gayfere had spoken about illness, mental illness.

"I see what you mean," said Pellerin politely. He wondered what mental disorder Gayfere was thinking of. It was obvious from his tone of voice that he was thinking of a particular complaint, perhaps of a particular case of it.

"The poor sufferer behaves in a way which seems strange, bizarre even," said Gayfere.

Pellerin cast a light, inquiring glance at him, and found Gayfere staring at him boldly. Pellerin, a little embarrassed, dropped his eyes.

Gayfere helped himself to another whisky and soda. Returning to his place in front of the drawing-room fire, he said, "Did you know that Dr Johnson was afraid of going mad?"

"I didn't."

"Boswell doesn't mention it as far as I can remember; he

only describes a few eccentricities of the great man. There are a lot of mad people about today." He paused and then added casually, "Mrs Shakeshaft's sister is mad, you know, and locked up in an asylum."

"Oh? I'm sorry. I hope she'll recover."

"There's not much chance of that, I'm afraid. They've tried everything except leucotomy—psychoanalysis, drugs, shock treatment. But Alice won't let them cut her brains out, so the leucotomy operation hasn't been performed. She says she has far too few brains as it is."

"Really?"

There was a silence for a while. Gayfere thoughtfully sipped his whisky. He was thinking of something that made him nervous, or so Pellerin thought from the expression of his eyes and his heightened complexion.

"Do you know," Gayfere said, looking beyond Pellerin and speaking with subdued agitation, "that Mrs Thrale would whip Dr Johnson whenever he felt he needed whipping." He paused, looked directly at Pellerin, and then continued slowly and emphatically. "That is to say that whenever he felt, at full moon or new noon, the rising tide of his madness, he would beg her to whip him—as an antidote, of course. This was the approved treatment of those days, a kind of 18th-century electrical shock treatment."

Pellerin made no comment. He had had the curious feeling that Gayfere was speaking to himself, and had almost lost sight of the fact that he was in the room.

14

To Pellerin's surprise, he found a fox's brush in Herbert's room. It was mounted on a silver holder and hanging by a ring from the wall.

"I didn't know that you hunted," he said.

Herbert blushed. "I don't," he replied.

Engraved on the handle, Pellerin saw, were the letters H.J.S.

"What does the letter J stand for?" he asked.

"Jeremy," said Herbert.

Pellerin read out: "Herbert Jeremy Shakeshaft. Bogshot to Wagstaff. 7 mile point. 8th November, 1952."

A look of helplessness came over Herbert.

"I was on a small pony," he said in a low voice, "and I didn't know that my mother had conspired to have me blooded that day. A groom we used to have suddenly seized the bridle and dragged the pony forward. The huntsman was surrounded by yelping hounds which were killing the fox. 'Ah, the young entry,' I heard him say."

He broke off his narrative for an aside: "It's funny how one remembers some things that are said ages ago, isn't it?" He continued with an expression of horror. "In his hand he had the fox's torn off tail. Before I knew what the horrid man was about, he'd pushed back my bowler hat and smeared the bleeding stump across my forehead and down each cheek, then dabbed it on my chin. 'There you are, Master 'erbert,' he said. 'Now you're a real fox 'unter.' I felt I was going to faint or be sick. I spent the rest of the day in a frightful gloom."

"And you've never hunted since?"

"No," said Herbert Jeremy with a shudder at the thought of it. He looked at the brush. "I keep that hanging there to please my mother."

"Bogshot to Wagstaff," murmured Pellerin, wondering what Mrs Shakeshaft, with her young son, and only recently a widow, had looked like on that day. "Was Gayfere there?"

"I think so." He paused. "He doesn't hunt any more because of his lumbago. He gets awful pains in his . . ." He hesitated. ". . . in his backside."

"Yes," said Pellerin, remembering that Gayfere had winced the other morning as he sat down to his eggs and bacon.

She is as cold as an ice lolly. She'll never know what my thoughts are about her, said Pellerin to himself in despair. At Christmas, he would go home, see Gladys of course, and in the herbarium gaze upon the heap of orders for Elixir of Life pills, aphrodisiacs, cures for constipation, warts, cancer, ear-ache, bad dreams . . .

And then? Of course, he would come back to Windwood, continue teaching Herbert Latin and Greek, see from the window Mrs Shakeshaft being borne away to the meet in her car in the morning, and hear the sounds of her return at dusk. She always rode back on the second of the two horses her groom took out to her, having worn out the first after three hours' riding. Pellerin calculated that she spent more time on a horse than in bed. No wonder she had such a splendidly slim figure.

She had the rare ability of warding off any waves of feeling that came from him to her. What a marvellous radar system she must have! It enables her to go underground as soon as she senses any danger. He wondered what part of her inviolable self she was trying to protect. Did he remind her of her late husband? What was the quarrel about, the quarrel which had split them apart? In those dark days Gayfere had stood by her side, advising her. Oh, he must have been filled with advice! Had it left her with a horror of men? Could she possibly be in love with Gayfere? The image of Gayfere made him reject this notion with a shudder.

He must ask Herbert to tell him more; but what, anyhow, would the boy know? He could only repeat that one day his father and mother had had a great quarrel, and add that he didn't know what it was all about.

Could Chauncy throw any light on the matter? What had he been on the point of telling him? His train had moved off before he could get the words out. Chauncy did not know what constellation of fears and pain existed in her, but he had learnt, apparently, of something which might supply a clue.

Suddenly Pellerin brushed all these thoughts aside. They were all untenable. She's just weak, lacks vitality.

As if to contradict this, he saw her in his mind's eye riding at a furious pace after the fleeing fox, a look of rapture on her face. No, no! whatever she lacks, it's not vitality.

15

The distant sound of a hunting horn, mingled with the cries of hounds, broke upon the air.

"I suppose," said Herbert to his tutor, "that it is a lot of money, but I don't see that it is going to make any difference to me."

"Not at the moment," said Pellerin, "but you may find that it will make a considerable difference to you in the future, and you'll be very glad of it."

They were following the hunt on foot.

Suddenly Herbert had found himself the owner of about a hundred thousand pounds; it had been left to him by his grandfather.

They came to a five-barred gate, got astride it and gazed down into the valley which stretched before them: they could see several of the field, moving with apparent slowness toward a copse, their bright scarlet coats making them appear like mounted ladybirds.

"They're going well," said Herbert with a critical eye. He pointed to two horses, one grey, one black. "There's mama; she's riding Cracker, her favourite."

Pellerin liked that. He'd not heard him refer to her as "mama" before.

"I hope the fox gets away," Herbert said.

He has identified himself with the fox, thought Pellerin. He feels he must escape, but how? And from whom or what? Not even his fortune is going to help him.

They began talking about Sir Roger Noakes, Mrs Shakeshaft's father, Herbert's grandfather, the son of the man who'd collected English and French landscape paintings (and one or two conversation pieces but nothing "modern"). He had left his daughter nothing; they had not been on the best of terms, because of one of those mysterious hatreds that spring up even in the best of families.

"I loved the old boy," said Herbert. The phrase "the old boy" was used with almost self-conscious awkwardness, a bulwark against sentimentality. "He was Master of the Hurlebat."

They clambered down from the gate and began walking towards the stream at the bottom of the meadow.

"Oh, he loved hunting!" exclaimed Herbert of his late grandfather. "He regarded the fox with peculiar affection."

"In spite of hunting him!" said Pellerin, his eyebrows rising with amusement.

"Hunting is different. If anyone killed a fox *unlawfully*, as he called it, he was furious."

"Do you mean with a gun?"

"By any means other than hounds. He read of a dog fox being burnt to death in a barn, and was shocked. My grandmother thought from the way he was talking that a school full of children had gone up in flames."

They both laughed at the eccentric old gentleman.

"I hurt his feelings awfully when I was a little boy. He took me for a walk on his estate one summer to show me a fox. I'd never seen a live one. Suddenly we stumbled on one in some bushes. To me it was only a reddish dog with a bushy tail. I said nothing. Silently we went back to the house. Later I learnt I'd committed a terrible mistake."

"How?" demanded Pellerin, anxious to learn the ways of huntsmen.

"I should have responded with whoops of joy." Looking round mysteriously and with an air of wonderment, Herbert exclaimed, "A fox! A fox!" He sighed and grew sad. "I should have pleased the old man; instead I hurt his feelings bitterly."

"But he forgave you," said Pellerin, thinking of the hundred thousand.

"We became the best of friends in spite of the fact that I don't hunt." Herbert fell silent.

They came to the stream and walked along it till they found a place to cross.

"Do you know," said Herbert, still thinking of his grandfather, "I feel I let him down badly."

"Do you feel that you've let your mother down badly too?" asked Pellerin.

"No, I don't," he replied. "Does that surprise you?" His large china blue eyes glanced up at Pellerin.

No, he doesn't love his mama, thought Pellerin, so he doesn't feel that he's let her down. Why? Was it because she didn't love him? Probably. Mrs Shakeshaft was too cold to love anyone. She was as cold as an ice lolly.

A hullabaloo suddenly burst about their ears: there were the hounds giving tongue as they raced by.

"Here they come," said Herbert gloomily as one of the field, on a big raking chestnut, came galloping up.

"But where's the fox?" said Pellerin.

"Thank God, I didn't see it," said Herbert fervently.

16

"I'd like you to keep the key of the cellar," said Mrs Shakeshaft.

"Certainly," said Pellerin, to whom the request was made.

"Mr Gayfere slipped going down there a year or so ago," continued Mrs Shakeshaft, "and he hasn't been down there since."

The key to the wine-cellar was handed over there and then. It was a big, heavy key, a delight to hold. Pellerin held it elegantly in his right hand.

The ceremony over, Wales departed.

Pellerin supposed that Wales was hurt that the key hadn't been handed to him. He had looked hurt in a stony, respectful way.

"I hope Wales isn't disappointed," he said.

"He's had the key for a year," Mrs Shakeshaft said. "But I think it far better if you took over that office."

There was a moment's silence.

"How is Herbert getting on? I hope you find him a diligent pupil. Is he clever enough to pass that examination? . . ." She broke off to search for the words.

"The G.C.E.?" said Pellerin.

"That's it."

"Oh, certainly. He should find it a walk-over at the Ordinary Level, at least."

"I'm very glad to hear of it, very glad indeed." Mrs Shakeshaft was conspicuously pleased. "But I don't think it necessary for him to sit for it, unless he wants to, or you advise it. He doesn't intend, I gather, to take up any of the learned professions."

"He's a poet," said Pellerin.

"I know," said Mrs Shakeshaft, a note of irritability appearing in her voice. She did not care, apparently, for Herbert's vocation.

Of course, thought Pellerin, it isn't necessary for Herbert, with a hundred thousand pounds, to earn his living; and there was his mother's fortune awaiting him in the future. He is a rich, although a sad, young man, and ill, alas. But why should she be irritated? Doesn't she like the idea of his being a poet?

"There's something else I should like you to do," said Mrs Shakeshaft, hesitating.

Pellerin was eagerly attentive.

She had never before related herself to him so purposefully; she'd only spoken to him in a vague, defensive way about the most conventional of things, so that he'd been forced to the conclusion that not only was she the coldest woman he'd ever met, but the dullest.

Pellerin gripped the key of the cellar, as if it were the key to her heart—a very big key for a very small heart—and waited for her to come to the point.

"How old is Herbert now?" she asked, as if he, of all persons, wouldn't know that.

"Fifteen and a half, I think," said Pellerin.

"Ah, is he?" said Mrs Shakeshaft, looking at Pellerin out of half-veiled eyes. "I thought he must be getting on for sixteen; there are the first signs of a beard appearing."

Pellerin hadn't noticed any signs of a beard appearing on his pupil's face, and he wondered if she were confusing her son's face with the face of another mother's son whom she met at the hunt. As he listened to her, a look of dissatisfaction came over him. She's fallen into her usual habit of talking, he thought, as if she's a stranger to all that goes on around her. Oh, well, if she's going to grow bored, so am I.

"Quite a young man, in fact," said Mrs Shakeshaft.

"Quite," said Pellerin, examining with cold detachment her marvellous complexion, so pink and clear, utterly different from her maid's complexion. He was reminded of a painting by Delacroix (not in the collection upstairs) of two harem beauties, one as white as Mrs Shakeshaft, the other as black as the inside of the chimney, and both as plump as capons. Mrs Shakeshaft was not that, but Beatrice seemed to be plumper and daily to grow plumper still, and her grey eyes deeper and more savage.

Mrs Shakeshaft had continued talking. For a moment, Pellerin thought he had misunderstood her.

"Sex?" he said, a startled look appearing on his face, as if she'd proposed the most outrageous thing. He knew nothing of that. What does she think?

She wanted him to tell Herbert about the facts of life. Was that why she'd given him the key to the wine cellar? Could there be a connection? Women and wine.

She was looking at him in surprise.

Pellerin took a firm hold on himself, gripped the key to the wine-cellar till the palm of his hand began to hurt.

"Do you think," he said off-handedly, "that this subject is part of a boy's . . . er . . . education?" (You might as well teach your grandmother to suck eggs.) Surely an intelligent boy like Herbert, who was a close student of natural history, who followed the seasons and the ways of animals, needed no special instruction on this score.

"I do indeed," said Mrs Shakeshaft.

"It's a large subject," said Pellerin, thinking of all the volumes written upon sex by Kraft-Ebbing, Havelock Ellis, Schrenck-Notzing, and casting, as it were, a gaze upon the cloud-capped peaks and sombre ravines of the perversions and anomalies.

"Is it?" said Mrs Shakeshaft with a sharp look.

"Yes," said Pellerin, wondering, with disgust in his heart, if he could take her on a tour of these Himalayas. He, a mere classical scholar, would be her guide, and point out to her, what unscalable peaks and gloomy valleys he would either leave out of the syllabus—for the feelings which engendered them were too curious, too rare, the creation of a quite impossible ideal.

"Any subject may be large, but the rudiments, surely, can be expressed in a few words."

He certainly did not want to explain this subject in few words.

"I suppose so," said Pellerin vaguely, thinking that, when she wanted to, she could be quite clever—she was, in fact, an intelligent woman. (But he'd never seen a book in her hand or even a newspaper, only a riding crop.) How mistaken, he thought grimly, one can be about people. One thinks this or that person superficial, stupid; then suddenly she grows intelligent, swells into significance.

It was not what she had said, but the manner in which she had said it that made him see her so differently.

Mrs Shakeshaft, thinking that she'd said enough on this subtle subject, left him with a forced smile. Pellerin still held in his hand the key to the wine-cellar, but he'd lost the key, or the clue, to her heart—he'd never really had it.

She's not afraid of death, he said to himself bitterly. She'd welcome it; she's not fleeing from anything when she's astride, but pursuing something. He wondered what. He pressed the key to the wine-cellar to his forehead. If only he knew.

He went upstairs, passing Beatrice on the way. She turned her olive-complexioned face, which was full of humility, towards him. He forced a smile to his lips and strode by.

He couldn't settle down to Anna Kingsford. His thoughts kept on wandering back to Mrs Shakeshaft and her request. Why should she assume that I know anything about the subject? I'm not a doctor. He decided that if Herbert himself had asked him a question or two on the subject of sex, he would of course reply to the best of his ability, and would not think anything of it. He would not treat it in any way differently from a question on Greek syntax. Why, then, was he upset? Because *she* had asked him.

It was her reply to the silent message which he'd been sending to her—"Go and talk sex to Herbert!" In some semi-conscious fashion, she had at last grown aware of him as someone who might fulfil another function in the house beside that of tutor, a function which Gayfere wasn't fulfilling—in fact, no one was fulfilling. She was adroit and perverse.

Chauncy was the fellow who should have explained these mysteries to Herbert, thought Pellerin indignantly, as he went down to the wine-cellar. He picked up the cellar book and with a morose expression began to inspect the entries. Afterwards he turned to the bottles laid out on racks.

When, an hour later, he came back to his room, he was quite clear about one thing. Wales had been helping himself. He had robbed his employer of several hundred pounds' worth of brandy and liqueurs. The bastard!

17

The cook was in a foul temper. She'd had a row with the butler, and threatened to leave.

"Just before Christmas, too," said Gayfere gloomily. "Sack Wales; we can always get another butler." He'd been into the kitchen and spoken to her in her native tongue—she was Austrian and huge.

She had gone to Mrs Shakeshaft.

"Madam, may I speak, please?"

"Yes, of course, Mrs Scheu."

"It is a very serious matter, affecting the right running of your house."

Mrs Shakeshaft grew most attentive.

"I've always been in good service," continued the outraged Mrs Scheu, "and the butler's room has always been done by the second footman."

Mrs Shakeshaft wondered what on earth was coming.

"I mean, ma'am, it is not delicate . . . You know, chamber pots and that sort of thing."

"Who does Wales's room?" said Mrs Shakeshaft sharply.

"Beatrice, ma'am. I don't think it's right."

Mrs Shakeshaft agreed with her.

Pellerin, who heard the details from Gayfere, did not like it either. No, this was not right. Wales will be sleeping with her next. Chauncy would be furious.

"You were quite right to speak," said Mrs Shakeshaft as she concluded the interview.

I'll wait a bit, thought Pellerin, before I have a word with him about the discrepancies between the cellar book and the wine.

Mrs Shakeshaft left the table, and the port began to circulate.

"I didn't know what she was in a rage about," said Gayfere, commenting on the event which had disturbed the peace of Bezill during the last twenty-four hours. "She wouldn't tell me. I thought she had gone off her head."

He fell silent. His expression deepened. Soon he was talking of the madness of George III.

"He was flogged as a cure for it," he said. He cut a pear in half, and began slowly to peel one of the halves.

"By whom?" asked Pellerin pedantically. He observed an expression of discomfort settle upon Herbert's face.

"His valet," said Gayfere, who was extraordinarily well informed on details of this kind. "His doctor was present, and he was in a straight jacket."

"I hope he improved under the treatment," said Pellerin drily.

"He did, he did," replied Gayfere, a light appearing in his eye. "That was why it was permitted."

Some people, thought Pellerin, are obsessed by foxhunting; others by flogging as a cure for variety of nervous complaints. Society accepts the one and regards the other as out of date, morbid even. Gayfere was not of this opinion. The glitter in his eye, the soft tone of his voice when talking on this subject, as if he were describing an elaborate ceremony, made Pellerin feel that there was something morbid about him. He wondered what deleterious effect his morbidity had upon Mrs Shakeshaft, for she surely absorbed something of it by the mere fact of living in the same house with him. "I didn't know that you were interested in unconventional cures," said Pellerin, thinking he should say something, because of the presence of Herbert.

Gayfere stopped peeling the other half of the pear, and looked at Pellerin with a startled, searching look. "Humani nihil a me alienum puto," he said in a tone which suggested a rebuke.

Pellerin turned to Herbert. "I don't regard anything human as a matter of indifference to me," he said, translating freely. He followed this with a brief comment on the construction of this sentence.

18

No, I was quite wrong in thinking she's afraid of death. It is not a matter of death at all, but of love and hate. She "loves" Gayfere—yes, even Gayfere—because Gayfere touches a chord in her heart, as it were, which neither her husband nor her father could touch. He, alas, was in the same boat with Captain Shakeshaft of the Blues and Sir Roger Noakes. That was why, Pellerin concluded, she is always so cold to me, as cold as an ice lolly.

He imagined her head carved out of pink ice—the pinkness of her lovely complexion—and himself as a hungry child with a tongue long enough for any story of the Grimm brothers. And then she began to cry tears as big as village ponds, melting away her lovely complexion . . .

Suddenly Herbert interrupted his silence with:

"Last night an owl cried in Beatrice's window. It woke me; it terrified her. And when she told me that it had screeched into her window, I was terrified too. She sleeps with the window wide open, you know, two hot water bottles, and a vast heap of blankets."

"Why?" demanded Pellerin. "Why should you be?"

He had not heard the owl himself, but then his window faced the other side of the house.

"There is a superstition in these parts that when a barn owl screeches into a window, the person inside will soon die."

"You don't believe that, do you?"

Herbert shrugged his shoulders. "I think it a bad omen," he said.

Pellerin was disturbed. "But that's absurd," he said. He cast a searching glance at his pupil. "She's a healthy young woman—bursting with health, in fact."

Herbert looked down at Charlie.

They were standing on the path at the back of the house, below the very window on the sill of which the barn owl had alighted and screeched, screeched, and screeched, until Chauncy's erstwhile mistress awoke from her heavy sleep, and with a fearful cry tumbled from her bed.

"She'll die," said Herbert simply.

"Are you a visionary?" Pellerin asked. Perhaps epilepsy and the capacity to see into the future went hand in hand. It used to be thought a blessed disease.

Herbert blushed. Without vision—of death, of life— the poet perishes. He couldn't help it. He didn't want her to die. Heaven forbid! But some are born to endless night.

Pellerin wondered if he should mention the matter to his employer, Mrs Shakeshaft. "Your son has visions of death. I felt I should tell you." But what would be the use of it? There were other things he felt like mentioning to her too, but he knew he wouldn't mention any of them. She was as she was: she rode to hounds; she very largely ignored her sensitive and ailing son; she hovered over the flabby but alert figure of her sombre companion, Gayfere ... (What was at the bottom of their sterile relationship?)

Pellerin was afraid that during the course of a lesson Herbert would start up, stammer a Greek word or two and fall down, foaming at the mouth and biting away at his tongue.

He felt like approaching Mrs Shakeshaft with a serious expression, a little sad perhaps, and saying to her without any preamble, "Your butler has been robbing you. Gayfere too; and you have been stealing from yourself. The absurdity of it all is more than I can stand." She would accept his resignation, of course, and he'd be haunted by the spectre of her ever afterwards.

His interview with Wales was a little less fanciful. He had, he explained, to bring these discrepancies to his notice, otherwise the blame of them might fall upon his own stewardship. Before mentioning it to Mrs Shakeshaft (he said this in a light and careless manner as if nothing untoward could possibly follow from it), he'd thought that he'd better explain what he meant, in order to save himself from appearing foolish. He knew, of course, that he wasn't likely to make himself appear foolish in any case; he was only making Wales look foolish, very foolish, and sorry, too, but he was not too sorry for him, for he did not intend, if he could help it, to pursue the matter to the end. It was of no advantage to him to see Wales sacked or prosecuted or worse. Mrs Shakeshaft was rich enough to bear the loss, and he could, he thought, so arrange it that she'd never know anyhow.

Wales, a big man, suddenly broke down. He didn't cry; he simply made a clean breast of it. It was not his fault at all, really, but his mother's—she was the culprit, and a dipsomaniac into the bargain. He simply could not afford to buy her the drink she demanded. Besides, the return fare to Ipswich was no trifle. Bottle after bottle he had taken her, intending, of course, to replace it out of his own pocket. He had replaced them to begin with, but then he'd fallen behind . . .

Pellerin tried hard to think what Mrs Wales looked like. He imagined her as a woman with not only a tremendous thirst, but of huge proportions—for how, otherwise, could her son hide behind her back?

Wales's remorse was getting on his nerves.

"The doctor has only given her another month to live." Something like tears had appeared in his eyes, but whether this was due to grief for his mother or for himself, Pellerin could not say.

"I'm sorry to hear that," he said, expressing conventional sympathy. "What is wrong with her?" As he asked this question he wondered if this mother of his existed at all. Wales had created her perhaps on the spur of the moment, and he was only now hurrying her into the grave because her imminent decease would sustain his promise not to take another bottle out of the house.

"She has cirrhosis of the liver."

"I'm not surprised," said Pellerin.

A flash of indignation, of rebellion, passed over Wales's face at this remark; it made Pellerin believe that he really had a dying mother. It was true then. Of course there is no reason why a butler shouldn't have a mother dying of cirrhosis of the liver, even if he has aided and abetted the complaint with gifts of cognac.

There was a short silence.

Should he feel indignant? Pellerin wondered. He certainly wasn't feeling indignant; it was not in his nature to feel indignant about such matters, and he wasn't even worried that the discrepancies between the cellar book and the bottles would ever come to light.

"What is annoying," said Pellerin, "is that your mother seems to have quaffed a lot of the 1875 brandy. I don't see why you should have given her the oldest brandy that was in the cellar."

Wales, who'd been cringing and sniffling, suddenly straightened up, and said with dignity, "Please, sir, don't forget that she is my mother."

Pellerin stared at him in perplexity.

An idea suddenly occurred to Pellerin, one of those simple ideas which are presented by the circumstances of the moment.

"How long have you been in Mrs Shakeshaft's service?" he asked.

"Twelve years, sir."

"Did you know Captain Shakeshaft?"

"I did, sir. A very fine man."

There was a pause.

"I can, of course, treat this whole matter as a secret, but . . ."

"Thank you, sir," said Wales, cutting in, a look of relief spreading over his face.

"I find it hard to believe in your ailing mother, but no matter." And looking up at the ceiling, Pellerin added philosophically, "One secret, I always think, is worth another. I'm sure there are many secrets of this household which you, after twelve years' service, have learnt about." His glance returned to Wales's face. "Don't you think?"

"Oh, there's nothing in the way of a secret that I know about, sir. I assure you, sir."

"Well, in that case," rejoined Pellerin, his expression hardening, "let's stop talking." And he moved towards the door.

"Sir! Just a minute," said Wales, stepping after him. "What is it you wish to know?"

Pellerin stopped and turned round.

"I don't wish to know anything," he said curtly.

"I'm sorry, sir," said Wales.

Another pause.

"There's nothing that you know that I can't find out for myself."

"Let me save you the trouble, sir," said Wales. "But tell me what you wish to know!"

Pellerin dropped the language of diplomacy.

"There's something that goes on between Mrs Shakeshaft and Mr Gayfere. What is it?"

Wales's face, it seemed to Pellerin, had grown, in the light of the unshaded electric bulb, a trifle green.

"He has a nervous complaint which requires an unusual form of treatment," he said.

"And the treatment is administered by . . . ?"

"Mrs Shakeshaft."

Pellerin felt sick.

"Let's go," he said. He stopped at the door for Wales to precede him. Chauncy's tennis-playing movements as the train had carried him away had become ludicrously clear.

19

"I know what I wanted to ask you, Mr Pellerin," said Mrs Shakeshaft, calling after him as he was going out to the terrace.

Pellerin, who had been behaving towards Mrs Shakeshaft as if she were no longer there, even at the dinner table, stopped and waited for her to speak. She was affable; her face reflected a look of amusement almost. "How did your little talk with Herbert go?" she said.

"It didn't," he replied. "I've not given it yet."

"Oh?" She affected great surprise.

"I've been waiting for a suitable occasion."

"Does it require that?" she said, looking perplexed.

"Everything requires the right occasion, the right time and place."

She didn't know what to reply to this; and he, not liking the strained silence, continued with, "There are young men, and young men. Some of Herbert's age would laugh up their sleeves at such a talk unless one took them, so to speak, on a tour of the aberrations."

He was conscious of having said something which, in view of the person to whom it was addressed, was audacious, indelicate even. He hardly dared to look at her. When he did so, he saw she was not looking at him, and her expression had taken on an almost frightened air.

"They know," he continued, "the broad, conventional outline of the subject already, and one would only hold their attention by entering upon bizarre forms; but there are other young men—Herbert is such a young man, I think,—whose minds are so delicately poised that revelations of this kind could do untold harm, especially if hurriedly presented."

"When are you going to tell him, then?" she said, speaking at last and looking at him with apprehension mingled with distaste.

"Soon," he replied with a smile; "and may I leave it until tomorrow to tell you definitely?"

"Of course," she said. And with this she left him.

He didn't think he would have anything definite to tell her the following day; it was just a way of concluding a tiresome conversation. Instead of informing her of his programme—the time and the involved circumstances in which he proposed to tell her son the facts of life—he felt like breaking his contract, leaving Bezill, and never coming back—no, not even for Herbert's sake.

How can she, he asked himself indignantly, increase the tension that already exists? To him, it was as if she'd said, "I'm only asking you to tell my son about the peculiar and (as I believe) *sordid* facts of life, because I know that you have been spying on me!" "But how illogical!" he exclaimed. (This remark was addressed to the Mrs Shakeshaft of his imagination—a simpler woman, not nearly so cold as the real Mrs Shakeshaft.)

It was only his intuition, his hunch, that there was a relationship, a positive link, as it were, between her asking him to talk sex to Herbert, and trivialities to her, while (behind the scenes) she relieved Gayfere of his psychosomatic sufferings. "She's not afraid of death; she loves it!" he muttered to himself. And he decided that the clue to her nature, which he'd been seeking since he'd arrived at Bezill, could be found in just that.

"Have you ever been abroad?" Pellerin said.

"Two summers ago, we stayed at Mentone," said Herbert.

"Did you like it?"

"Yes." He was silent for a while. Then he said, "There was a girl there. She was with her mother. She seemed very proud."

"Did you speak to her?"

"Oh, no," said Herbert. He found the idea startling. "I would see her on the beach. She was older than I."

This is the first time, thought Pellerin, that he has referred to the opposite sex. Had it, he wondered, any special significance?

"In what way was she proud?"

"When she saw me looking at her, she tossed her head in the air."

"They do that," said Pellerin, as if women were horses. "Would you like to go abroad again?"

Herbert turned a questioning gaze at him.

"An educational tour round Europe. Just the two of us."

"Yes," said Herbert, "I would. I would indeed."

"I will ask your mother," said Pellerin.

The idea had come to him furtively, a fragment of an idea at first; it was not there when he had asked himself what he was doing with Herbert, and if his brief lessons had any meaning for either of them. Yes, that was what he really would like to do, to take Herbert abroad "on an educational tour." It would be an insult to Herbert, and to himself too, to expound the facts of life at Bezill in the prevailing circumstances—the circumstances provided by his feelings towards Mrs Shakeshaft, and of the nature of her relationship to Gayfere, a relationship which sprang, he thought, from another relationship, that between herself and her recently deceased father whom, he gathered, she had abhorred. A love-hate relationship in both cases, especially one of hate, as great a tie as love. No, no, there was no question of his telling Herbert about the facts of life—and of death, especially death, the death of the unborn child, so to speak—here at Bezill, or at any old place. No, their thoughts must be composed, and the longing of their respective hearts stilled—his for Herbert's adorable mother who was held in a clasp as cold as an ice lolly, and Herbert's for the girl who tossed her head proudly when she observed him gazing at her, or for another perhaps. He foresaw himself pandering through the brothels of Europe (or at least through some of those that still existed in these reformed times and had not been shut down by governments alarmed at the new teaching), expounding to the poet Herbert by practice as well as precept the mysteries of sex. Geoffrey Pellerin was nothing if not thorough. But would Mrs Shakeshaft agree to it? He thought she would, especially if he found a suitable way of putting it. And by suitable, he meant a way which would compel her to agree, for nothing must be left to chance, to the whim of a cold, cold woman. The proposal, in other words, must fit into her own plans, if she had any. It was no good his thinking that, to succeed, he had only to create a situation in which she would want him out of the way, or then she would only dismiss him. No, he must bring her round to seeing that he was essential to her son—his health, his joy—if not to herself, and that his going away was only to return—at a time not too far distant when things would be different. But why did he want to go away? He turned over a letter he'd received that morning from Gladys, the usual kind of letter from her. She sent him news of the herbarium, of the addition of a new cure for asthma which Raymond had recently added to his list. It was made from a herb of the "Chinese Ephedra Tree: the remedy with a 4,000 years reputation," to quote from the leaflet which she had enclosed. She invited him to spend Christmas with her. *Now that you've gone away, I regret all the opportunities I've lost in being sweet to you.* The letter fell from Pellerin's hand on to the desk. *Be assured*, he felt like replying, *you lost none*. But the thought of so much sweetness lost persisted, and began to fascinate him. Should he go up to Mrs Shakeshaft—she was probably in her room at the moment—and tell her simply that he loved her too much to allow this mockery to continue. What mockery? Wasn't it mainly in his own imagination? And if he burst in upon her, he'd only find Gayfere there, in a straight jacket, bound to the end of the bed, and Mrs Shakeshaft playing tennis in the alcove.

It would be easier to take Herbert to Pompeii and Heraculaneum and show him the frescoes which depict scenes of conjugal life; and to the Museum Eroticum Neapolitanum for phallic monuments and gimcracks. Yes, he must broaden Herbert's mind, enlarge his education, lavish his heart with indefinable pride.

22

The sound of a woman's voice—not Mrs Shakeshaft's, but that of one of her guests—floated through Pellerin's open door and fell with this sentence on his ears—a sentence torn from its context as far as he was concerned by her rapid passage along the corridor.

"I met him at the Wire Fund dance."

He wondered what the Wire Fund dance was, decided that it had something to do with hunting: barbed wire was anathema to hunters. So she had met him at a dance, but what happened after that? Pellerin did not know; he hoped that neither of the two people concerned had any regret. He returned his thoughts to the novel he was reading.

Later Beatrice appeared in the doorway which led to the bathroom next to his room, and stopped short. From her wild gray eyes she cast a frightened look at him, turned and was gone.

He rose from his chair and called after her. "It's all right, don't run away; I'm going."

He was disturbed at the sight of her figure. She's always hiding from me. Why should she be afraid of me. Does she think I'm Chauncy? And he went after her.

She was there, behind the bathroom door, a duster in her hand which, like her face, was olive-complexioned.

"Do go in," he said gently, standing on one side.

He followed her to pick up the novel and depart, leaving her to make the bed and dust or do whatever she wanted.

She stood awkwardly, apprehensively, dumbly, in the

centre of the carpet, as if, Pellerin thought, pleading with him not to rape her. (She was in enough trouble already on such a score.) He looked at the outline of her full, firm bosom and, for the third and last time, exonerated Chauncy, but condemned his timidity. Pellerin should have met the two of them at the station and seen them recede together as the train drew away, making with their free hands (the other they were clasping) the movement of tennis players.

"What is that?" she said, stretching out her hand till her fingers rested on the surface of the novel: she ran them along the title.

"It's a Portuguese novel."

She was artless, naive, a wondering child.

"Can you read it?"

"Yes."

She was not surprised; he could do anything.

He waited for her to say something else, but she was silent. He wanted to speak to her, but found himself tongue-tied. He couldn't, he realized, start praising her, telling her what a nice looking girl she was, and advising her to learn shorthand or domestic science perhaps, equip herself with a diploma and wander off to London.

He had never before seen eyes like hers. What streams and genes he wondered had mingled there? Her teeth were as strong as a bear's, and quite regular. She must have been under the care of an excellent St Helenian dentist, or had they just grown like that?

Pellerin began to retreat, leaving her to work. A look of anguish appeared on her face; she made a movement towards him, her lips parted. He hesitated, waited for her to speak, but she said nothing. A sadness came over her eyes. She had left him, he realized. He took the opportunity to escape.

23

"I suggest we go to Holland, catch a boat from Rotterdam and sail down the Channel, leap off at Lisbon and work our way through Europe from the south-west corner. There is a marvellous museum of carriages, unique of its kind, in Lisbon."

Pellerin unfolded his plan: from Lisbon they would board the Lusitania Express, bed down for the night, and wake up at nine in the morning in Madrid. He told Herbert of the wonderful portraits by Velasquez of court dwarfs and fantastic sketches of witches and succubi by Goya in the Prado. As he mentioned succubi, he wondered if that might not make a nice point of departure for his sex education talk, succubi. Had Herbert been visited by any? The purple rings round his eyes suggested that he had been, that they consorted nightly with him, and were draining away his manhood. What of the pretty little French girl, who tossed her head with newly awakened vanity, and awareness that she was a prize most earnestly sought? Perhaps on their travels, they would meet another such girl, one a little older, with hair tied horse-tail fashion. Pellerin was of the opinion that young men and women should find companionship in each other.

Herbert was enthusiastic; then he grew thoughtful and quiet for a moment. "But what if my mother won't agree?" He stared at Pellerin, his face full of unhappiness at the thought that nothing might come of these projects.

"I think she will, you know."

"Have you mentioned the matter?" Herbert asked eagerly, hopefully.

"Not yet."

Herbert said nothing, and the look of unhappiness returned.

Pellerin grew anxious: he should not have aroused these expectations. What if they were not fulfilled? His outline of the tour had included, of course, Italy and Greece, especially Greece, the home of Pan. With a start, he realized that he must succeed in persuading Mrs Shakeshaft to agree to the tour, otherwise a dullness would come over his relationship with his pupil. He must take Herbert away. He needed to be taken away for his health's sake. Of course, Herbert knew nothing of Gayfere's nervous complaint which was, so to speak, impinging upon his own complaint, but can anything be wrapped up and hidden away? Does not the sensitive mind perceive everything in some secret fashion? Pellerin was of the opinion that Herbert's epilepsy was largely, if not wholly, due to his mother's hatred of her father, Herbert's grandfather. Thus the sins and omissions of one generation fall on the backs of another, and drag them to the ground. Mrs Shakeshaft, whose photograph astride Cracker, her favourite, had appeared in *Country Life* (with a pleasant smile stuck on for convention's sake) was a woman isolated, frosted up. She kept everyone, her son included, away from her: no wonder Herbert had fits, could not go to boarding-school, had to have a tutor and was growing up a dunce.

"Why doesn't Mr Gayfere get his lumbago cured?" asked Herbert, as if he'd read Pellerin's thoughts. "He can hardly sit down. He's taken to a rubber cushion." Herbert smiled, but it was no smiling matter, really.

"Who blows it up for him?" asked Pellerin, wishing to change the subject.

"I saw him hand it to Beatrice and tell her to blow it up for him."

"No!" exclaimed Pellerin. "Beatrice?"

"Is that wrong?" Herbert looked questioningly at his tutor.

"I suppose not." But Pellerin, in his heart, was disgusted to think of Beatrice's breath sustaining the flabby frame of Roger Gayfere, egoist, epicure. How cruel the world is! A film spread over his eyes; he averted his head from his pupil, and walked away.

24

"It will do him good," Mrs Shakeshaft said to herself, and expected in a vague way to see some remarkable transformation in her son—the result of enlightenment. But there was no transformation and no enlightenment.

She couldn't understand why Pellerin had not told her when he would broach the delicate subject. It was clear that he was reluctant. She wondered why. He was behaving in a somewhat strange way.

The expectation of a remarkable transformation in Herbert's manner and appearance—in the complexion of his skin for instance—was her own idea, not that of the Harley Street physician who had confirmed the suspicion that the boy was an epileptic.

It was an odd idea, indeed, more odd than Pellerin's reluctance to put it into practice, but this had not occurred to her. Pellerin, for his part, after wondering for a day why she had suddenly asked him to switch from Greek to sex, had decided in his own mind that it was, as it were, only her muffled reply to his anxious glances in her direction, a diverting of his attention.

But whatever her reason, her ultimate reason, he was left with the problem not only of where he was to begin these lectures—he'd decided that—but how. He was reminded of *A Problem in Greek Ethics*, an essay written in late Victorian times. Should he approach the subject, so to speak, invertedly? (No, he thought not, for Plato had strongly condemned that sort of thing in *The Laws*.) Should he treat the whole matter as an extension of the hour's Greek lesson? The Greek way of life, Pan, Priapus.

He was listening to Gayfere holding forth on herbs, their great value in cooking, especially in connection with soups.

Pellerin, who had picked up a thing or two in Raymond Pasquier's herbarium, extended the discussion from herbs as flavouring for food to herbs as cures for everything, including lumbago.

He saw that Gayfere was looking at him abstractedly, and for a moment Pellerin wondered if he were saying something absurd or, what was worse, betraying a vulgar interest. He was not to know the meaning of this abstracted stare, while he held forth on the medicinal properties of plants, until some time later.

At that moment Mrs Shakeshaft's voice was heard.

Pellerin rose from his seat as a pretty woman with dark hair and brown eyes and a lively expression appeared. As soon as she opened her mouth to reply to Mrs Shakeshaft, who immediately followed her, Pellerin knew that she was the person who had met someone at the Wire Fund dance.

"I never hunt in the Friday country," said Mrs Shakeshaft. "It's all wire." This remark disturbed Gayfere from his reverie. He began to get up from his seat, revealing the air cushion which Beatrice had inflated for him.

"Mr Pellerin: Lady Skrymsher," said Mrs Shakeshaft, introducing them.

"How do *you* like the Friday country," said Lady Skrymsher.

"I'm not sure where the Friday country lies exactly," said Pellerin.

"Mr Pellerin doesn't hunt," explained Mrs Shakeshaft.

The embarrassment which Pellerin was beginning to feel was fortunately cut short by the appearance of Commander Skrymsher, a young local farmer, the owner of a herd of prize coypus, produced entirely by artificial insemination; or could it have been long-haired goats or short-horned cattle? Pellerin was not quite clear on the point.

He had grown so friendly with his pupil that, at times, he felt like confessing his worries to him, not all his worries, but some of them, the lesser worries.

"What do you think of Commander Skrymsher?" he asked Herbert.

"Oh, I like him," said Herbert, a reply which aroused in Pellerin faint resentment. "He's a sport."

In what way he was a "sport," Pellerin did not inquire. He wondered if the Commander, whom he did not like, was born under the obstinate and unprepossessing combination of Leo and Taurus: his appearance suggested that.

Gayfere was sitting painfully on his air cushion.

At his age (Pellerin had decided that he was in his early sixties), he had only one duty, namely to his literary memories, his recollections of famous writers, like Frank Harris, André Gide, Thomas Hardy, which he must generously pepper with anecdotes of lesser writers. But why must Beatrice blow up his air-cushion for him? Why can't he blow up his own air-cushion? Pellerin imagined that he was short of breath, like those people who are short of cash and have to ask for a loan.

25

"Well, now, Mr Pellerin?" said Mrs Shakeshaft, giving him a questioning look.

He realized that the moment to unfold his Tour of Europe plan had arrived.

He did unfold it, there and then, and as naturally as if he were proposing a tour of the picture galleries in London. "I thought of taking a boat to Lisbon, of leaping ashore and from that ancient and splendid city beginning our wandering . . ."

He broke off, savouring the happiness of the expression "leaping ashore"—yes, from the lanes of the Tagus in bright winter sunshine. Oh, what happy wanderers they would make, what a splendid effect it would have on the development of Herbert's character, what fine poems he would write . . .

"I couldn't agree to anything like that," exclaimed Mrs Shakeshaft, interrupting the flow of Pellerin's thoughts, tying them up in a bundle, so to speak, and tossing them away.

Well, that's that, thought Pellerin, in dismay. He couldn't argue with his employer.

There was a silence for a moment or two, and the only comforting thought he took from the disappointing situation was that Mrs Shakeshaft wanted him near her, in constant sight, because, in some mysterious way, he was necessary for her existence. (Or perhaps it was only that Herbert was necessary for her existence, but that was hard to believe.)

He hadn't yet told her the purpose of the proposed tour; in fact, he'd put the whole matter rather clumsily. Should he try again?

"If I may say so, Mr Pellerin, a trip abroad, as you suggest, would make a very nice holiday for Herbert, and for yourself, but I hadn't anything like this in mind when I engaged you to teach my son . . ."

"Of course not," cut in Pellerin, feeling embarrassed.

". . . and frankly I am rather surprised that you should suggest it."

Pellerin stared at her uncomfortably. She, at any rate, had had the courage to speak her mind. She was surprised. He felt a resentment growing inside him.

"Is it all that surprising?" he said with a certain aloofness. "I only want to show Herbert some of those places which figure in our lessons—Rome, Athens, Herculaneum—so that they will take on an aspect of reality for him." And he added with a touch of irony before she could reply, "I should have thought that such a tour was inevitable sooner or later."

"But you mentioned Portugal," she replied, slightly confused.

"I didn't intend that we should stay long in Portugal, and if one is going to the Continent, one might as well see some of the lovely cities of Portugal—Cintra for example, which Southey called the most beautiful in all Europe."

"I see," said Mrs Shakeshaft, finding (Pellerin supposed) the proposal not quite so outrageous as she had at first thought. "And how much would it cost?"

"A cool figure," he replied.

There was a momentary silence.

"I'm afraid I don't know what a cool figure is," she said distastefully. And added with a little ironic laugh, "It sounds like slang to me."

"A cool figure is a thousand pounds. I haven't gathered it is slang." The phrase, he thought, reflected his own coolness which since the start of this conversation had fallen upon him. A cool figure. There was something cool about Beatrice's figure.

"Oh, I couldn't afford that!" Mrs Shakeshaft exclaimed.

Pellerin reflected that when wealthy people say that they can't afford this or that small sum, they mean it; it might be only one pound but they can't afford it. A sort of financial constipation comes over them.

He wished the conversation would cease, but she seemed in no hurry to stop. Another silence ensued.

"How is Herbert getting on? I was glad to hear that you think he could pass the G.C.E."

"Admirably well, I should think," he replied, not at that moment particularly caring if he would pass "admirably well" or not even pass at all.

"I'm so glad," replied Mrs Shakeshaft in a lifeless voice. She was groping for something that she wished to say. Pellerin waited. "And how did your little talk with him proceed?"

As he did not reply at once, she added, "on the facts of life," as if her meaning had not been entirely clear.

Pellerin had been expecting this question, but when it came it still made him start slightly. The solitary word "What?" broke from his lips.

Mrs Shakeshaft repeated her question.

"Your talk to Herbert on . . . on . . . on sex. How did it go?"

"It didn't," replied Pellerin, watching the look of disappointment break over her face. "Frankly, I don't think Bezill is the right place for such a talk."

"Why not?" she asked with an expression of alarm. "Why isn't Bezill suitable?" Her eyelids narrowed as she looked at him.

"Why?" he said, clasping his hands together. He sighed instead of replying. It would be difficult to tell her why. In the first place he wasn't sure; and in the second place, he didn't choose simply to do what she told him to do in this connection. He felt like telling her quite frankly that he had read Homer and Virgil but not Havelock Ellis and Freud. Sex meant nothing to him, and he was the last person in the world to impart such instruction, especially at Bezill, with the butler stealing the brandy, and betraying all her secrets. In other words, couldn't she see that he was in love with her?

She was tired of waiting for him to continue.

"I could do so in Greece perfectly easily but not here." And before she could comment on this, he was talking to her about Priapus and fertility rites, the moral of which was that the lesson would naturally develop along the lines she desired when they stood before the statue of the erect god.

"This is all too roundabout," she exclaimed. "I can't follow you."

"Then you won't agree?"

"No, I won't agree."

"Oh, well, in that case . . ." said Pellerin, feeling that he should take a stronger line with her, but at a loss to know how to finish the sentence. Fortunately, she did not wait for him to finish the sentence.

"I shall have to think about it," she said.

Would she really think about it? It was a disturbing idea. Was this an indication that she no longer cared for him? if she had ever cared! And did he really want to go away on the continent with Herbert?

"How long do you expect to be away?"

"Six months." He would not stretch out the time. He could promise her that.

"It's a long time, isn't it?" she said. "Really, you surprise me, Mr Pellerin."

"I surprise myself," he answered, rather unhappily.

She had no comment to make on this irrelevant remark.

He was not going to rush round the galleries of Europe like a tourist who has half an hour to "do" the Louvre, and a whole day in which to see Rome. He looked reproachfully at his employer. He did not believe that she was really going to consider his proposal; she was only talking in this way in order to appear reasonable.

"There was nothing about going abroad for six months in our arrangement," she erupted plaintively.

"True enough, but then the subjects you asked me to teach did not include biology," he replied promptly, if a little impolitely.

"And must you go abroad to teach that?"

He was thoughtful for a moment or two. "Yes," he said. "Yes."

26

A fall of snow. Seasonal weather, but unsuitable for hunting. The meet, in fact, was cancelled to Mrs Shakeshaft's irritation.

Pellerin was looking out of the window of his room, watching a robin on the path below. Christmas is coming, he said to himself. Another letter from Gladys, inviting him to spend Christmas with her in the herbarium lay on his table. It had arrived that morning. A vision of a "turkey", made of flour, nuts and seasoning, and swamped in some brown vegetarian sauce, rose before his gaze. "Don't you find it irresistible?" she wrote ironically. She is mocking me with mock turkey, but what have I to offer her but mock love? The robin turned quickly and flew off. Fly away robin, fly away love. Herbert's spaniel, Charlie, coming round the corner of the house, had frightened cock robin; and Mrs Shakeshaft, coming into his life with equal suddenness, had driven away his love for Gladys, if love was not too strong a word for the emotion he had felt for her.

He would, anyhow, spend Christmas Day with his parents, and descend on Gladys perhaps for cold mock turkey on Boxing Day. Would they—stubborn vegetarians that they were—warm up the crumbling remains of a moulded turkey on Boxing Day? And would the sight of Gladys warm up his heart so that it would beat for her as it used to? What an excellent wife Gladys would make; that, he had to admit.

The spaniel began barking; a pheasant, strolling across

the snow-covered lawn, began to fly, long-tailed, towards the wood.

Half an hour later, Pellerin was walking with a volume of Donne in his pocket, along the tree-bordered road. The night's fall of snow had been heavy, but it was already melting in the sun. He took the volume of Donne, an old one, from his pocket, and turned the pages.

> Goe, and catche a falling starre,
>   Get with child a mandrake roote,
> Tell me, where all past yeares are,
>   Or who cleft the Divels foot . . .

Get with child a mandrake roote—the mandrake which shrieked when pulled from the ground. It was a "nonsense" line, but it produced a powerful image. Get with child . . . Beatrice had gone out last night and not returned.

Mrs Shakeshaft was the first to learn that she had disappeared, for the girl had not come into her bedroom in the morning with the tea-tray, drawn the curtains back, handed her her bed-jacket, shut the window, announced the time. For Mrs Shakeshaft, it was most disconcerting.

At breakfast, Gayfere had expressed the opinion that she had gone to London to find her lover Chauncy. He was in a jocular mood.

Mrs Shakeshaft stared hard at him. "This is the first time I've heard that Mr Chauncy is, or was, Beatrice's lover," she remarked lightly.

Teach me to hear Mermaides singing.

They were probably in bed together at this moment, thought Pellerin, and he looked reverentially up into the cloud-decorated sky.

She had wanted to say something to him the other day. Her lips had trembled; she had been on the verge of speaking. Doubtless she wanted to ask his advice, show him, perhaps, a letter from Chauncy.

But an angel had whispered into her ear, Go and catche a falling starre.

Was Mrs Shakeshaft also like those monkeys who see, hear, and speak no evil?

A running stream brought the snow to an abrupt end; it sparkled in the sun, wandered through the wood.

A fallen tree provided a bridge. On the other side was the silent wood in its winter sleep.

Pellerin suddenly stopped before a holly tree clad in green leaf. What a fool he was! He should have shown enthusiasm for hunting, then she would have mounted him at least once a fortnight. What fun he could have had galloping after her! No, it would not have been fun. In pursuit of the unattainable.

He set off along a path through the wood. Bogshot was on the other side. He would walk to Bogshot. *Bogshot to Wagstaff*.

The tracks of some four-footed animal in the snow led to the edge of a dark pool, and disappeared. It was a fairly large pool, and fairly sinister. In the centre was an island, planted with defiant trees.

How absurd of him to have made a barrier between them by his indifference to the only thing that gave her pleasure, the chase.

A swan glided into view from the other side of the island, and approached a bundle floating in the dead rushes. Pellerin wondered what the bundle was; he went nearer and clutched his breast as he saw that it was a corpse. He wondered vaguely what it was doing there. A moment later he realized, with a feeling of horror, that it was Beatrice. He could not see her face, but he knew that it was she.

Her dress had split open, exposing a protuberant belly, as tight as a drum.

The supercilious swan unfurled its neck and sailed towards him.

His feet, it seemed, had grown into the earth.

Suddenly he tore himself free, and plunged into the water which rose immediately to his knees. The swan swept away, hissing.

He dragged the body to the bank, propped the head with its ashen face, against a moss-covered tree, and ran off, breathing loud.

He had thought of ripping up her belly, of snatching the child from the bowels of death, literally from such bowels.

Get with child a mandrake roote.

But he hadn't a penknife.

She had been wearing stays, concealing as well she might, Chauncy's handiwork.

27

Pellerin had run off as if speed was the essence of the matter, as if some frantic effort on his part might yet save the situation; but before he had got far, he realized that the girl was dead. It was her belly, not her face, which had been above the level of the water.

By the time he reached Bezill, his pace had slowed down to a walk, a slow, sad walk. It was a cold, crisp day, and he was soaking wet, but he did not feel the cold, and was not very aware of his clammy clothes.

Well, he must tell somebody, he said to himself as he entered the house. It was not something to keep to himself. And they could tell the authorities. He flinched from the ordeal of telling Mrs Shakeshaft, who was at home this morning. It was a choice between Wales and Gayfere. He decided upon Gayfere, and made for his study.

"Come in," said a voice which he recognized as Gayfere's—voices, if not faces, had grown unreal to him, such had been the shock of finding Beatrice dead.

He went in.

Gayfere looked up, said "Hold on a moment, will you?" and went on writing. Pellerin had interrupted him in the middle of a sentence.

It seemed to Pellerin to be a very long sentence, especially as (he supposed) he had interrupted him when he had been half way through it, one of those interminable sentences that long-winded writers love.

"Hallo, Pellerin," said Gayfere at last, laying aside his pen. "What is it?"

Pellerin stared at him from unhappy eyes, and found himself unable to say anything immediately.

"Well?" said Gayfere, his smile vanishing.

"Would you mind getting up and coming over here, sir?"

Gayfere's expression changed to one of perplexity.

"What is it? You've interrupted me. I am writing my memoirs."

"I am sorry. I have my reasons."

"Good god, you're dripping wet."

"Please come over here." Pellerin beckoned him.

Gayfere thought for a moment that Pellerin only wanted to show him from the window something odd that was taking place in the garden, but there was something a little too odd about his manner. Suddenly Gayfere felt afraid. He did not know why. He measured the distance between himself and the door.

"What is it?" he said, getting up, and giving a fearful glance at the window.

To his amazement, he suddenly saw Pellerin dart forward and seize his inflated rubber cushion from the seat of his chair.

"What on earth are you doing?" said Gayfere in a loud terrified voice.

Instead of replying, Pellerin let the air rush out, pressing both sides of the cushion with his hands.

"You can't keep her breath locked up in here. She's dead. *Pneuma*, the Greek for the spirit, is the same word as for the wind. The wind that rustles the leaves and stirs the waters of the deep. Let her spirit go, for goodness' sake." He looked reproachfully at Gayfere.

To his surprise, he saw Gayfere rush through the door, and a moment later he heard him calling wildly for the butler.

28

After lunch, Wales told him that Mrs Shakeshaft wanted to see him. (He'd not seen her since breakfast.)

Pellerin was writing a letter to Gladys at the time, a confused letter—he was in no mood to write to Gladys; he couldn't get Beatrice out of his mind. (He told her about Beatrice, about trudging back with the local police to the pool, and being interviewed by them.) As for Christmas—well, he'd come and spend Boxing Day with her, thank you very much. *Sorry I didn't reply to your letter before the last, but I've had a lot of things on my mind.* And I still have, he thought.

"If only," he said to himself out loud, "she had spoken to me. She was on the point of doing so; she had almost opened her lips . . ." He wondered if there was anything in his face which had prevented her from telling him all, seeking his aid. He got up from the table and went to the mirror on the wall.

At that moment, Wales knocked on the door.

"She's in the Blue Room," he added, after he had told him that Mrs Shakeshaft wished to see him.

As Pellerin went down the staircase to confront Mrs Shakeshaft in the Blue Room, his face was set with a grim, determined expression. He said to himself, Don't parley with her. Leave at once.

He expected her to upbraid him for tearing the cushion away from Gayfere—had he torn it away?—and of blaming him, perhaps, for Beatrice's suicide. To the first accusation, he would reply with bitter laughter. And why does he need an air cushion? Tell me that. He foresaw the colour in Mrs Shakeshaft's face draining away at this remark. He expected words, arguments, dismissal.

"Come in," he heard her say immediately after he had tapped on the door of the room she used as her private sitting-room, as if she had been anxiously waiting for him.

He turned the handle and went in. She was standing, white-faced and worried, beside the chimney-piece.

He had already told her that he'd seen Beatrice, her maid, rotting in a sinister pool beside an unruffled swan—until he had plunged into the water and ruffled it—and she was not, he felt, going to reveal to him any anxiety on that score by asking further questions.

"I've decided after all that it would be a good thing if you took Herbert away to the Continent on the educational tour. When do you want to leave?"

He was pleased to hear her use his phrase—educational tour.

"Whenever it is convenient," he replied.

"As far as I am concerned, as soon as possible."

"But how about the inquest?"

"Don't worry about that. The coroner may be cross, but I don't care."

"I'm surprised that you've changed your mind," he said with a little forced laugh.

"Why shouldn't I change my mind? Don't you?"

He stared at her, amazed at her composure, at a loss for words.

"Go to Cook's in London. Take Herbert with you, and make all the arrangements. Put up at Brown's Hotel. I always stay at Brown's. My bank will supply you with all the money you need." She paused, then added. "How long do you want to stay away?"

"I don't know," said Pellerin, a little dismayed.

"Don't come back under two months at least. If you run out of money, let me know in time, and I will see that you get more. I don't want you to stint yourselves."

He heard himself murmuring, "Thank you, Mrs Shakeshaft."

He found Herbert amid the trees in the park, seated on the trunk of a fallen beech. He was throwing a ball for Charlie to catch.

"We're going abroad," he said.

"I know," said Herbert.

There was a short silence.

"But aren't you glad?" asked Herbert. "I am."

Pellerin was not glad. He didn't want to go away now; he wanted, more than anything else, to talk to Mrs Shakeshaft, to talk to her for days, weeks, to tell her that she was leading an absurd life, and that if she had any sense she would consider him as a prospective candidate for her hand. Et cetera. Yes, et cetera.

"I'm glad," said Pellerin, not wishing to undermine Herbert's enthusiasm. "I'm very glad."

"It's marvellous!" said Herbert.

"I was suddenly summoned to the Blue Room . . . but there's one thing that I can't understand." Pellerin hesitated.

Herbert took the ball from Charlie's mouth and threw it far; then he returned his attention to his tutor.

"She seemed in a hurry to get rid of me—of us!"

Herbert had no comment to make on this, especially as Charlie had returned with the ball.

It was growing dark. The breeze knocked one branch against another of a nearby tree. Signal to depart.

"Let's go," said Pellerin. "The sooner we get away, the better."

They walked in silence towards the house.

29

The letter he'd written to Gladys, he'd torn up and written another, one more to the point—a different point, for his plans had altered. He was not going to eat cold mock turkey. The prospect had brightened. He would probably eat his Christmas dinner on Christmas Eve, and in another country.

So, dear Gladys, expect one of those delightful colour postcards from me; indeed, a succession of delightful colour postcards as I wend my way, with my pupil, through Europe . . .

He did not tell her the nature of the educational tour he was going to conduct. It was no good entering into such delicacies with Gladys. She was too straightforward a person, and probably an extrovert.

He pondered on how he should deal with the matter. His relationship with his pupil was a sensitive one—Herbert's mind was finely differentiated. He refused absolutely to approach the subject from the angle of animal biology, to unfold it with the bluntness of those educationalists who believe that "the truth" justifies the means. He toyed with the idea of unfolding his theme in allegorical form, as a union of opposites, an alchemical wedding, between the male and female principles, symbolized by the sun on the one hand and the moon on the other.

A knock on the door interrupted this train of thought.

"Come in," he called out.

The door opened and Gayfere appeared.

"Ah, here you are," he said light-heartedly. He closed the

door carefully behind him, and advanced into the room.

"Forgive me for intruding on you like this," he said, "but as you're going to London tomorrow there isn't much time."

"Am I going to London tomorrow?" Pellerin looked at Gayfere in surprise.

"I understand from Alice that you're going off tomorrow morning."

"Oh, perhaps I am," said Pellerin. Yes, perhaps he was. He must ask Wales; Wales would know. He didn't want to ask Mrs Shakeshaft anything any more. Yes, they were to stay in Brown's Hotel in London. Had their rooms been booked?

"I want to ask you a very great favour," said Gayfere.

"If I can do anything, I shall be happy to," replied Pellerin, gazing at Gayfere guardedly, and not wishing particularly to do anything for him.

"Thank you," said Gayfere, throwing his head back and stroking his neck. He was having some difficulty in coming to the point.

Pellerin cast his eyes to the carpet, and did not raise them again until he heard Gayfere speaking. The first sentence he did not properly catch. It contained a reference to Pasquier and his herbarium. The second sentence was surprising but clear: Gayfere wanted aphrodisiacs.

Gayfere's face was straight, even solemn.

A startled, almost amused look broke from Pellerin's face. He tried at once to suppress it, and succeeded. All that was left was a keen, attentive air.

"Would you write to him for me and ask him? I mean, since you know him, it would be easier for you."

"Certainly," said Pellerin, trying now to be as casual as he could. He didn't mind in the least helping Gayfere in this way. More business for Raymond. He was sending his aphrodisiacs all over the world. There was no reason why he shouldn't send a packet to Bezill.

"As a matter of fact, I'm writing to him at the moment," said Pellerin.

"Oh, good," said Gayfere. "Well, would you mind telling him to send me his strongest variety and as soon as possible, and enclose his bill."

"Right, I'll do that."

"You don't mind?"

"Not in the least."

Gayfere began to retreat. He'd said what he'd wanted to say. He mustn't take up more of Pellerin's time. "You won't forget, will you?" he said, standing by the door.

"Of course not." Pellerin seized his pen and another sheet of paper.

"Thank you very much. This is a favour I won't forget."

Gayfere had gone.

Pellerin wondered why Gayfere wanted these herbal restoratives. It was no business of his, of course. Perhaps he wants it as an experiment. To see if, in his old age—how old was he? Probably no more than sixty-five—he could still get the sap to rise. A curious experiment to make.

30

"I was up last summer. Not a good Gaudy—only three Garters at High Table."

Well, that's pretty poor, thought Pellerin, who was sitting on a sofa beside the French window in the drawing-room. With a feeling of relief, he watched Mrs Shakeshaft and Commander Skrymsher pass out of sight.

So she has other interests, he thought. He could talk to her about Oxford and its grandeurs, too, if she would give him a chance. He wondered if she'd been up at Oxford. Of course, he hunts, he's the Hunt Secretary, and that makes all the difference. Pellerin, who'd never been on a horse in his life, felt quite miserable. He'd missed his chance all right, when he'd told her that he didn't hunt, and implied that his philosophy of life prevented him from hunting. What a fool he'd been! Had he identified himself too closely with Anna Kingsford? (He'd been neglecting her of late.)

"Oh, here you are!"

Pellerin was awakened from his reverie by Mrs Shake-shaft's voice. He got up from the sofa as she came through the open French window, and a defensive mood descended upon him.

"I've been looking for you."

"I've been sitting here," said Pellerin, trying to appear innocent, as good as gold.

"I'm going to a party tonight, so I'd better say good-bye now, and good luck. I hope you and Herbert enjoy yourselves."

She was actually smiling at him.

"You won't, of course, forget the purpose of your trip?"

"I don't usually forget what I have to do," he replied ungraciously. "I suppose you're thinking of the sex talk?"

"Yes, what else?" she replied stiffly. "I think it's important, especially as I'm getting married next month."

He wondered what she was talking about, getting married? To whom? He looked at her in amazement.

"I'm sorry you and Herbert will be away then," she said, looking distantly at him.

"May I ask if it's anybody I know?"

She gave him a quick glance. "To Mr Gayfere," she said, affecting surprise.

A sensation of horror spread itself throughout his body; with an effort of will he tried, but failed, to suppress it.

"Perhaps it's for the best," he said.

"What?" said Mrs Shakeshaft.

"That Herbert and I shan't be here."

She was silent for a moment; then, with a smile, which this time was forced, she said, "It's odd you should say that, for that's what I've been thinking."

It seemed to Pellerin that the time had arrived for a little plain speaking; it was now or never. Moreover, it seemed to him that she, in some mysterious way (as she drew near to the brink) wanted him to speak to her plainly.

She is isolated, he said to himself, cut off by her feelings from everyone, and she is appealing to me to help her.

"Do the facts of life matter?" he asked her. "And what are they?" He paused, and then rushed on determinedly. "What is life, anyhow? Hadn't we better decide that before getting down to the facts of life? And whose life are we talking about? Is it your life or your son's life or mine? You have your life and he has his. Of course he should know at his age the facts, and I will teach them to him to the best of my ability, but aren't you confusing the planes when you think these facts should be learnt in time for your marriage. I mean, after all, he's not marrying you!"

"That's a very odd thing to say, Mr Pellerin."

"Is it odd?" He paused for a moment. "I don't find it odd. I find it obvious." He glanced at her with an expression which did not encourage contradiction. "You are getting married and he must be told the facts of life—don't you see the connection? And I have to tell him."

"There is no connection," she said firmly. "And why shouldn't you tell him? Who could be better?" She seemed surprised.

"You don't see the point."

"I'm afraid I don't," she replied calmly.

"Has it ever occurred to you, Mrs Shakeshaft," said Pellerin bitterly, "that I might be the worst person to talk to Herbert on such matters?" (He didn't think he was.)

"You mean because you are not married?"

"It's true that I'm not married, but I wasn't thinking of that."

"But I thought that that made very little difference today among young people," cut in Mrs Shakeshaft before he could tell her what he was thinking of—not that he intended to tell her.

"I am not married because, until recently, I had not met anyone I cared to marry."

"Until recently?" said Mrs Shakeshaft, pronouncing these words with incredulity.

"Yes."

She was afraid to ask him to be more explicit or to tell him that these personal aspects of the matter, as far as she could see, were none of her business. She could only think: he had not found, until recently, anyone whom he would care to marry. And who was it he had found now? Was it

Beatrice, a woman who was no more, who had changed his mind for him? Or herself perhaps? It was possible but she was not interested in following the complexities or rather the vagaries of his mind that far.

She gave him a wan smile, raised her eyebrows, and went off without another word

He was reminded of his letter to Gladys, which lay unfinished on the table in his room. He hadn't asked her to send Gayfere some strong aphrodisiac. Five minutes later he had the letter before him. He wrote:

Another matter. Will you please send to Percy Gayfere Esquire at this address a good anaphrodisiac, sodium bromide, I suppose. Put on the label, To be taken two hours before required. He, poor man (or lucky chap, depending on the way you look at it) is suffering from satyriasis, won't leave his wife alone, is the terror of the female servants, wants something to quieten him down. Make it strong. N.B. Don't say on the bottle what it is. Tact is necessary, above everything.

No, he was not, after all, going to help Gayfere. On the contrary. The image of Mrs Shakeshaft, her face transfigured by a sad, imploring look, was borne to him on the wave of imagination and desire, and was a reflection of a similar imploring, sad look on his own face: it was all, he knew, too late. He had had three months during which to woo and win her, and he'd won nothing.

31

"We are taking the same route as Sophie von Laroche," said Pellerin as they reached Harwich. "She was a friend of Goethe, you know. She visited Sheraton's workshop, also Wedgewood's in 1786. There is a delightful account of Wedgewood and his china factory in Sophie's memoirs . . ."

Herbert did not seem to be taking it in. They went aboard ship. On the night trip across the North Sea, Herbert slept very well.

Welkom Thuis
Welcome to Holland

"That's nice," said Herbert, pointing.

Now they were on a train, going to Rotterdam. It was pitch dark outside. They had the carriage to themselves. Pellerin thought they might as well go straight to Rotterdam.

When they arrived there, a clerk from the shipping company informed them that their ship—of the Swedish South East Asia Line—was late; it had been held up by fog in the Baltic.

They spent Christmas Day in Amsterdam.

"I love Holland," said Herbert. He was enthusiastic about the windmills and the canals.

They wandered through museums, gazed at Rembrandt's *Night Watch*, and a roomful of paintings and drawings by Van Gogh, arranged according to the places in which he'd done them: Paris, Arles, St Remy, Anvers.

Pellerin told Herbert about the noble Dutchman, the painter who cut off his ear for a woman.

Herbert's comment: "Must one do that?"

He's guessed, thought Pellerin, the underlying motive of this trip, and sees it as a sacrifice of blood.

They returned to Rotterdam, and the following morning a gentleman from the shipping company called for them, and took them in a chauffeur-driven car to Nieuwe Maas where a splendid ship lay waiting for them.

"What a lovely sight," said Herbert, gazing at the forest of masts and funnels—ships of all nations at anchor or being moved about.

A vast brown cargo boat passed them close, hooting its boisterous warning. Ships went by them all the time.

During the late afternoon, the pilot came aboard, and in the fading light two tugs drew them towards the sea. A huge floating crane passed alongside. Herbert, who'd remained on deck, gazed up at its winking lights.

The river widened. From the shore a church bell tolled. Flares from high masts spread a garish light over the river bank. Ships and lights slowly disappeared.

Four days later, they came out on deck to see the ancient town of Lisbon across the water—white and red and blue-grey buildings rose upon the hill, and sparkled in the morning sun. The two travellers were filled with joy. Winter had been left behind. There was Portugal. Now for their adventure!

32

He unfolded his plan to the boy who leaned, with bowed head, against the jamb of the chimney-piece. And when he had finished, the boy raised a white, startled face to him, opened his mouth to say something, make some comment perhaps on what his tutor had said, but fell silent instead, his face flushing with emotion.

The mysteries of sex could only be revealed by practice, a personal demonstration in which the novice, the learner, is the demonstrator. (One of two.) Live and learn; love and learn. The only way to learn about love is by loving.

"That, in a nutshell, is what I suggest," said Pellerin, moving one leg from under the other. He was lying stretched out on the bed.

"But where," asked Herbert in a febrile tone of voice, "is the . . . the . . . the woman?"

"Fortunately," replied Pellerin with a smile, "that presents no difficulty in a place like Lisbon." And with a gesture towards the window of the hotel bedroom, he added, "For here brothels abound."

"Oh," said Herbert. "Oh." And fell silent.

It occurred to Pellerin that Herbert might not know the meaning of the word *brothel*. What, as a matter of interest, was its etymology? He thought it came from an Old French word meaning *ruined*. Yes, ruined. Was he ruined? He didn't feel exactly ruined. Perhaps that was because he'd only been to three. And what a good thing he'd been to those three, for otherwise he could hardly recommend them to Herbert—as an educational institution, that is.

He decided from Herbert's thoughtful and almost embarrassed silence that he had grasped the meaning of the word.

"I must confess, dear master," said Herbert at last, "that what you propose fills me with dread."

"Dread?" said Pellerin, sitting upright with surprise. "Well, if you are filled with dread, let's scrap the whole idea. You're obviously not ready for this kind of thing."

"Oh, please don't misunderstand me," said Herbert. "I *am* filled with dread at the thought of it, but that, I think, is only right; for how else should one approach such a place?"

Pellerin jumped off the bed. He'd understood. "How right you are! Dread was the frame of mind in which the worshippers entered the great temple of Eleusis. Dread and hope, for the mysteries were about to be revealed." Embarrassed by the strength of his feelings, Pellerin turned his back on Herbert, and stared ruefully down into the street—at a woman in colourful rags who carried a basket of exotic fish on her head, her face hidden from his angle of vision.

He turned back to his pupil. "Can you go through with it?" he asked.

Herbert did not reply immediately. He looked up at Pellerin, an expression of frankness and sorrow in his large china blue eyes.

"Yes, I think so." His voice was so low that Pellerin only just caught the words.

Pellerin took from his pocket a packet of French cigarettes, and extracted one. He was relaxed about the whole matter. "Do you want to?" he asked. It wasn't for him to force his pupil, even for strictly scholastic purposes, into a house of ruin. There were limits to education. One could drag a donkey to a well, but getting it to drink was another matter.

At that moment Herbert looked as if he found it hard

to breathe. Was it, wondered Pellerin, that he did not wish to reveal his hidden desire, thinking that his moral stature would thereby be reduced in his tutor's eyes? If he is thinking along those lines, Pellerin said to himself, he is mistaken. I haven't set foot on the continent of Europe with any such preconceived notions.

But Herbert was not thinking along those lines; he was thinking along other lines, lines of imagination and grandeur.

"Dear master," he said, "may I beg a favour of you?"

"Yes, Herbert," said Pellerin cautiously; he felt slightly apprehensive.

Again Herbert fell silent. Then, with difficulty, he began to speak.

A startled look appeared on Pellerin's face, and he riveted Herbert with his gaze. Herbert had asked him, in a voice of tender supplication, that when they arrived at the place, at the house of ill-fame, of ruined hopes and fortune, that he should introduce him as an English lord. Just that.

"What on earth for?" said Pellerin.

Herbert bowed his head in confusion.

"The question," said Pellerin, "is superfluous, I suppose. I don't mind." And he dismissed the subject from his mind. But a moment later, he asked, "Lord who?"

"What name would you suggest?" asked Herbert, his poise regained, relieved that his master had seen the point, and more or less agreed with it. He tried to think of a suitable name.

"Lord of the Isles?" suggested Pellerin.

Herbert smiled and shook his head in swift short motion.

"Lord Shakeshaft?"

No: Herbert did not like that either.

"The only difference it will make is that they'll shove up the price," said Pellerin sombrely.

A look of pain passed across Herbert's face.

"What's the matter?" asked Pellerin.

"I can't bear to think that money is involved."

Pellerin did not reply to this. He retired instead to the bed and stretched himself out again. He still held a cigarette in his hand. He put it in his mouth and lit it. He blew out a cloud of smoke. "Anyhow," he said at last, "I'll settle up. You can forget that side of it, but I do suggest you give the woman something—a tip."

"How much?"

"If she pleases you, be generous." A look of indecision on his pupil's face made him add, "But don't overdo it. Give her a hundred escudos."

"I wish I had a gold sovereign or two," said Herbert wistfully.

"Don't be so old-fashioned," replied Pellerin.

It was three o'clock in the afternoon when they started out from their hotel. Pellerin had found out from the clerk at the reception desk the address of a high-class establishment. It was not far away.

The sun was shining. There were glad expressions on the faces of the well-dressed, respectable people in the narrow streets. He himself was not exactly feeling glad, due to the weight of his responsibility. He would much sooner have sat in a café and watched life go by, but he had his duty to perform. He reflected that the life of a tutor was irksome at times. Would he be expected by the patronne to take his fill of the fare? He wasn't really in the mood. He sighed. Herbert, walking close to him, looked quite sombre. Perhaps he should have a word first in the girl's ear? Fortunately he knew Portuguese, not too well, but enough to make himself understood. And afterwards he would speak to the girl again. Or was this superfluous? Mrs Shakeshaft wouldn't ask him for any details. Really, he was like one of those swimming instructors who fling the pupil into the water with the command, "Now swim!" Moreover, if he were engaged in the same pursuit in an adjoining closet, he wouldn't be available to instruct his pupil in anything.

"I think we're here," said Pellerin, looking round. They were in a courtyard with a fountain in the centre. Above was a line of windows hung with red curtains.

"Through here," said Pellerin, entering an open doorway. They ignored a hunchback girl who was peeling an orange, and began to mount a dark, wooden staircase, that was shining and smelling of a recent polishing. They stopped before a tall oak door, studded with iron bosses.

As Pellerin tugged the ancient brass bell-pull, a deep apprehension (or a look of gloom perhaps) appeared in Herbert's eyes.

Nothing happened.

"The place seems very quiet," observed Pellerin.

He pulled again on the handle.

"I only wanted to speak to her," said Herbert. "I wouldn't have annoyed her. I would have done everything in my power to please her,—run messages for her, bought her ice cream . . ."

He was talking about the little French girl he'd seen at Mentone two years ago.

"The girl with the horse-tail hair," said Pellerin, as he pulled the bell handle again—hard and long this time.

He thought he knew the kind of woman Herbert would like. A young, slim woman, hardly more than a girl, with her hair done up in horse-tail fashion.

"It's not the hair," said Herbert wisely, "but who wears it."

Suddenly a light appeared near the centre of the door: a small panel, at eye level, had opened, and a man's voice, speaking in Portuguese, demanded to know what they wanted.

"To come in," said Pellerin. He did not like the face he found staring at him, especially the flattened nose and the upper lip with its vicious scar. "My companion is Lord Bolingbroke."

"We're closed. You're too late for today."

"But Lord Bolingbroke . . ." began Pellerin, vexed.

"Lord Bolingbroke or no Lord Bolingbroke," cut in this prize-fighter, "we're closed. Come tomorrow." And with this, the light was suddenly cut off with a thud: he'd slammed the guichet.

"What did he say?" asked Herbert, not having understood a word—apart, perhaps, from "Bolingbroke" which the doorman repeated as if all his teeth had been loosened in the effort.

"We've come on the wrong afternoon," said Pellerin, turned round and facing the dim stairs.

"Oh, bother!" exclaimed Herbert in a lively voice, a voice in which Pellerin detected relief—immense relief.

They went down the stairs. The hunchback girl moved out of the way for them as they reached the bottom. She had by now eaten her orange, and looked at them with an air of vacant surprise. Pellerin strode out into the sunny courtyard, with Herbert following a few paces behind.

Suddenly a woman's voice shattered the peace:

"*Toma lá, filhinho, e não bufes!*"

And the contents of a chamber-pot, aimed at Pellerin's head, crashed down. Just in time Pellerin flattened himself against the wall.

"*Filhos duma puta!*"

The line of windows with red curtains were crowded with jeering, laughing women, women with bare bosoms who shook their fists in the air and hammered on the window panes.

They all shouted at once:

"Que raio de gajo é que ele julga que é, lorde de merda?"

"Ora o paneleiro do lorde!"

"E quem é o coiro do outro choninha?"

"Só se me fizesses um botão de rosa, filhinho!"

"Que vão para a puta que os pariu, os bifes, os lordes de merda!"

"Come on!" shouted Pellerin, flinging his arm in the direction of the exit, and glancing back at Herbert at the same time.

"Vá para o caralho!"

Herbert had wisely retreated into the shelter of the doorway, but at this command, he emerged and fled through the courtyard after his tutor while the contents of another chamber pot and a silk slipper rained down. The slipper caught him on the shoulder, which lucky shot brought an explosion of laughter from above.

Half way down the street, they slowed down to a walking pace. Herbert was out of breath.

"What on earth was the matter?" he gasped.

Pellerin was laughing.

"What were they shouting? Please tell me," begged Herbert.

"Henry Bolingbroke, Duke of Hereford," said Pellerin gravely, "I beg you to excuse me from translating such vile remarks." He looked sorrowfully at his pupil. "Your title upset them. We have arrived too late. The eighteenth century is over. The English milord is no longer respected as he used to be. We live in degenerate and absurd times—not even Portugal has escaped the wind of change."

"I thought it had something to do with my silly pretensions," said Herbert humbly. "We can't go there again. Even I can understand the *lordes de merda!* bit."

"Thank God," said Pellerin fervently, "you don't know more Portuguese than that!"

There were, Pellerin reasoned, other such establishments in Lisbon, or one at least which did not have its half-day holiday today (so that the employees could do their shopping, go to the pictures, or out with their boy-friends, and make love like the rest of mankind).

"They should have put a notice on the door: Early Closing on Thursdays," said Herbert.

Pellerin could see his pupil having a nightmare tonight unless the unhappy events of the afternoon were effaced: angry women hurling abuse, and worse, at English aristocrats was a fairly good basis for night terrors with so sensitive and tender a person. So after dinner he told Herbert to get his coat; and they went out again. In Pellerin's pocket was the address (given to him by one of the night-porters) of a place which was noted for its specialtés de la maison. They went there by taxi, and were admitted immediately by a negro with broad shoulders.

"He's a bouncer," said Pellerin.

"Bouncer?"

"Yes, he bounces people out."

Herbert, who was about to ask another question, fell silent at this.

"Only those who are kicking up a fuss," said Pellerin.

A bent old man who was waiting behind a counter in a recess lined with green silk took their coats and bowler hats; the hats he handed to a small boy who ran off with them round a screen, a serious expression on his little face.

Herbert saw a number of coats and cloaks hanging up

from wooden pegs (and three silk top hats on a shelf); but of course they were not the only customers (and how many coats and cloaks, top hats, and walking-sticks were behind the screen?). The thought made him feel sick at heart.

At the foot of a carpeted staircase, they were met by a young woman, pretty and well dressed, who invited them into what could only be described as a reception room. Herbert, for a moment, was left behind, looking at a bronze statue of a satyr on the terminal of the bannister rail. It was about eighteen inches high, in an attitude of pursuit, erect and leering. The young woman turned round for him, smiled as she saw the gaze of awe on his face. Herbert was so innocent.

The walls of the reception room were lined with large mirrors which tilted downwards from the ceiling. A clear space was in the centre of the polished parquet floor—for dancing, Herbert supposed as his eye alighted on a record player, the first modern thing he'd seen in the place. The friendly young woman invited them to sit on the sofa, or to select one of the upholstered arm-chairs.

They all sat down, and the young woman produced a silver cigarette case, and offered it round. Pellerin, who was talking to her in French, took a cigarette; Herbert, too, although he didn't usually smoke, and did not even wish to smoke on this occasion, but it was only a mechanical action, all his thoughts being absorbed by a painting on the wall. It was one of those wildly romantic frescoes which, with a certain omission, might decorate a gay, but entirely respectable, night club: its subject was two naked figures facing each other, and bound by cruel ropes. The man, in the full vigour of his manhood, was struggling like mad to get to the woman, and the woman was struggling like mad to get at him, to consummate their passion—only a few inches separated them at the nearest point.

Herbert wanted to ask, "What does it mean? I don't understand. Please explain it to me." But in the presence of the young woman, he remained silent, and tried to puzzle it out for himself. He decided that the figures depicted were not criminals, caught, and going to be tortured; the bonds were solely symbolic bonds, inhibitions imposed by society, or by God, and that these two frantic persons were only torturing themselves with their desires. They wished to overcome the moral restraints imposed on them, but it was impossible. Hence their agony. The central feature of sexual feeling was thus revealed to Herbert Shakeshaft. He had received his first lesson. With a shudder he turned away.

Suddenly there entered the room a tall handsome woman; she came up to the two Englishmen with a glad smile as if they were old friends of hers.

"How do you do?" she said in perfect English, offering her hand to Pellerin, and then to Herbert, to whom she gave one of her charming smiles. "I'm so glad you managed to come."

"It's a great pleasure," replied Pellerin with a slight bow.

A feeling of embarrassment seized Herbert. They'd obviously come to the wrong place. How else could one explain these airs and graces? This lady was expecting guests, and believed they were the guests. It was a private house. He wanted to nudge Pellerin and whisper "Let's go," before they grew more involved. How simply awful. Thank god she didn't know their secret purpose. She'd be deeply insulted. But Pellerin seemed perfectly happy, chatting away about the weather with this fashionably dressed woman with a lovely bosom.

"Did I not see you two years ago in Lisbon?" she said.

Instead of replying with words, Pellerin who seemed in an excellent mood laughed lightly, his eyes closing in sheer delight.

Herbert's gaze again took in the painting on the wall. How incongruous it was, really, in this respectable home. The young woman by his, Herbert's, side was obviously the daughter of the lady who was speaking, and yet they did not look alike. It was a little dreamlike. Suddenly the lady with the lovely bosom said, "Now I expect you would like to meet some of my children." Pellerin's smile vanished, and his face took on a serious expression. The feeling of incongruity, of dreaming, ceased immediately. Even Herbert, who had not yet reached his sixteenth year, did not expect to hear the sound of childish laughter and to be greeted halfway up the stairs by the capering offspring of this charming woman: her children had, he was afraid, a world-weary look behind their smiles and innocent, carefree manner.

"Well, madame," replied Pellerin, "we are primarily spectators."

Herbert wondered what on earth Pellerin meant.

"Ah, as you say in your tongue—'the looker-on sees most of the game,'" she replied immediately. "Now, I wonder what we can do? In room number forty-one . . ."

"Oh, no, madame," cut in the younger woman. "Do you remember he takes an hour to start and our friends here probably have other engagements."

Herbert was surprised that she, too, spoke perfect English, but the meaning of her remark was so beyond him that had she spoken in Turkish he would not have understood less.

"Well, in that case, room eighteen."

Her beautiful smile reappeared as she turned to Pellerin and Herbert again. "Come," she said, and led the way out of the room, and up the stairs.

They proceeded along a carpeted corridor, the walls of which were hung with Renaissance-style oil paintings of love feasts, works in the manner of Boucher, and nudes in all manners.

Madame stopped before a door, and laying a finger on her lips for silence, opened it and invited Pellerin and Herbert to step inside.

"Go in," said Pellerin to his pupil, and added something in Portuguese to Madame, who replied in the same tongue with a look of understanding. Herbert entered alone, leaving them still talking in a whisper.

He found himself in a small room, dimly lit, the walls of which were hung with old French prints, finely engraved and subtly coloured. There were eight of them, all on the same theme, that of a chamber maid, armed with an enormous clyster—*Das Klystier*—and on the point of administering it to some grande dame who was in the appropriate position to receive it. One of these prints was called *Le Curieux*, a title which referred to the male spectator who discreetly watches the maid at work. Until that moment Herbert had not even known of the existence of such an instrument as a clyster. He wondered what was being pumped into these splendid ladies who seemed to be treating the whole matter with fortitude.

He glanced through a small window let into the middle of one of the four walls, a window so devised that one could see through it from one side only, Herbert's side. A sofa was set before it. He sat down and looked through the window into the adjoining room. After a while he could make out a figure there. It was a woman. She was young and pretty. Now, she was getting undressed. Herbert began to feel a curious sensation in the region of his loins. It made him feel worried.

There was a man in the next room too. He was also undressing.

Herbert glanced towards the door: it had almost closed. He could partly see Madame, and could hear Pellerin. What on earth was he talking about? The baroque in art, apparently. Why didn't he come in and sit down and explain what was happening in the next room? Suddenly he saw something which filled him with repulsion, then amazement. He couldn't stand it any more. He staggered up. He burst out of the closet. "It's Mr Chauncy!" he cried in a whisper. "My old tutor!"

Pellerin darted into the closet. The broad face of Henry Chauncy, distorted by an expression of ferocity, glared for a moment in his direction.

Pellerin returned to the passage. "Yes, it's certainly Chauncy," he said. "But it's not as odd as you might think. You see, he told me, when I met him on the platform at Swanbridge, that he'd always be one leap ahead of me!"

Madame discreetly closed the door of the closet and, shrugging her shoulders, led them up to the floor above.

Pellerin, it seemed, had not only been talking to Madame about the baroque in art; he'd been telling her about that little French girl whom Herbert had seen at Mentone, she who had proudly tossed her hair in the air.

"I've just the person," said Madame. "Room thirty-six."

And it was to room thirty-six that they made their way after fleeing from Chauncy. Pellerin was rather sorry not to take advantage of this chance meeting to let him know how his poor mistress had suffered and died. It would bring him to his senses.

Herbert was trying to shake off the image of his former tutor, especially his ferocious, and perspiration-covered, face. It was horrible, horrible!

If only he had had a penknife, thought Pellerin. He might have saved the child. Should he hang about till Chauncy had finished and then tell him? He was almost certain not to know the sad fate that had overtaken Beatrice. But what was the use? It was all too late, too late!

Before the door of room thirty-six to which Madame had led them, Pellerin said, "I'll be waiting for you downstairs."

"Don't leave me," Herbert whispered.

This was unexpected. For an hour at least that afternoon Pellerin had spoken to him about the nature of coitus (he preferred the Greek word). It was a union of opposites, sol and luna, brother and sister, hot and cold, gold and silver, round and square, the physical and the spiritual—quite a lecture on alchemy, in fact, certainly enough for him to go confidently forth and discover the hidden treasure in room thirty-six. Madame had assured him that she was no more than nineteen and had a horse-tail style of hair-do.

"She will remind you of someone," Pellerin said.

"Of whom?" said Herbert with a look of fear.

Should he put his head round the door, Pellerin wondered, to see if room thirty-six did really contain a suitable person for so sensitive a youth, one who would make up in understanding and gentleness what she might lack in innocence. What an awful thing it would be, if, by some error of memory, Herbert was thrown to one of those frightful women who are found in all large cities, women who hate the men they prey upon, and who have overlarge breasts and dark hair upon their upper lip.

The door of thirty-six suddenly opened to interrupt these meditations.

A young woman, a mere girl of fifteen or sixteen, with long limbs and golden hair stood naked before them.

"*Alors quoi! Tu entres ou pas?*"

As the furiously blushing Herbert did not reply, she took him by the hand and pulled him inside. The door slammed. With a sigh of relief, Pellerin walked away.

34

Pellerin went slowly down the stairs, thinking of the alchemical marriage which was beginning to take place in room thirty-six. He reached the first landing. The prince and the king's daughter . . .

Madame was waiting for him at the foot of the stairs, smiling up at him, doubtless preparing to ask him which of her children he personally would like. Should he? In such a place, one might as well . . .

Suddenly a loud cry rang out from above. A look of alarm descended upon Madame's smiling face, and she clutched the lascivious satyr on the bannister terminal.

Pellerin halted, turned and ran back. Oh, my God, what's happened? That was no ordinary cry.

With equal suddenness, a woman screamed: it was more terrifying. A door was flung open with a crash, and the voice, growing louder, cried, "*Madame! Mon client a des convulsions! Madame! Mon client a une crise!*"

Within seconds, Pellerin was in the room, and on his knees beside his pupil who was lying on the floor with a blue face, the veins of his neck swollen, the pupils of his eyes huge. Pellerin thought he was choking. But what could he do? Shouldn't he prevent him from biting his tongue off? But he wasn't biting anything.

He looked wildly about the room, espied a little whip on the dressing-table.

"Give me that whip," he said to Madame as she rushed into the room with a look of alarm, followed by the naked girl.

Herbert's legs began to jerk violently, his mouth opened and closed—too soon for Pellerin to thrust the ivory handle of the whip in—and his breath was blown out in short puffs.

Slowly his face resumed its normal colour and the movements of his limbs ceased.

"He's recovering," said Madame.

"*Pauvre garçon*," said the naked girl. "*Il était si gentil.*"

35

He informed Mrs Shakeshaft by cable of what had happened, and within hours received a reply. He and Herbert were to return as soon as possible. She seemed annoyed as well as alarmed.

After the fit, Herbert had fallen into a deep sleep, and did not leave room thirty-six till the morning. Pellerin slept in the adjoining room, and in the arms of Madame herself. She had offered him a choice of several ladies of the establishment, but he had declined them all in her favour. Owing to the unusual circumstances attendant upon his visit, she had agreed to this.

Herbert made a rapid recovery. Forty-eight hours later, apart from a slight bruise on the side of his face, he looked quite normal, and behaved as usual. Pellerin saw no reason to rush back to England.

He sent a coloured picture postcard to Gladys.

At Cintra, he sent another cable to Mrs Shakeshaft, telling her that in view of Herbert's recovery, he thought they should return leisurely.

Mrs Shakeshaft wired back: DON'T COME ON TUESDAY TWELFTH.

They left Portugal. Pellerin felt (by a rare intuition) that Herbert had been on the point of asking him to take him back to see the girl with the horse-tail hair style, and the tender impatience; and Pellerin couldn't quite approve of that in the circumstances.

The train to Madrid rushed through the night, bearing

them away from Madame and her siren child. They were in the Spanish capital on the twelfth (January). Pellerin was restless the whole day, and melancholy by nightfall.

Yes, he would return to Bezill, and then leave—in disgrace, with Gayfere sneering at him through one of the upstairs windows. Gayfere would say to the next tutor, "We had an awful fellow here called Geoffrey Pellerin—a libertine and a perverter of youth."

She had wantonly closed her eyes to the facts, the "facts" about him (while he had opened her son's eyes to other facts). "But I am not mocked," he said out loud to his reflection in the looking-glass in his Paris hotel room. (This, because he had just read in *The Times* an announcement of her wedding to Gayfere.)

As the Channel came in sight, Pellerin's thoughts began to dwell increasingly on Anna Kingsford—would he ever finish his account of her? Really, full-time tutoring made the writing of books very difficult.

Down below were green fields in tidy lots; they were flying over England now.

"Will my mother be at the airport to meet us?" Herbert asked.

"I hope not," said Pellerin. The thought shocked him. He planned to go to Brown's Hotel, and talk to her first on the telephone—if she was there to talk to, and not honeymooning in Scotland or Germany. He would offer her his resignation; he need not return to Bezill or ever see her again.

Later that day, after they'd arrived at Brown's Hotel, checked in, rested on their beds, taken baths, and had had something to eat, Pellerin plucked up courage and rang Bezill.

Wales answered the telephone.

"Mrs Gayfere's residence," he said.

"This is Mr Pellerin," said Pellerin, feeling sick. Mrs Gayfere! "Can I speak to Mrs Gayfere?"

"Well, sir," said Wales cautiously, "you can, but . . ."

"But what?" said Pellerin sharply.

"Mrs Gayfere has lost her voice."

"Laryngitis?"

"I shouldn't say it was laryngitis, sir, but shock."

Pellerin felt a stab of fear. God, had she taken it so badly? Well, it wasn't his fault. Herbert was an epileptic, and had been one before he came to tutor him. Perhaps it was misplaced enthusiasm which had made him take him to a Portuguese brothel, but how was he to know that he would have a fit there? If he'd known he was going to do anything like that, he wouldn't have taken him there; he'd have taken him elsewhere—to a circus perhaps.

"It's been a terrible shock, sir," continued Wales.

"I can understand that," said Pellerin, "but, after all, was it entirely unexpected?"

"Entirely unexpected, sir, I can assure you of that."

"But he had had a fit before," said Pellerin, irritated.

There was a pause.

"Oh, sir, you don't understand. I'm referring to Mr Gayfere's death . . ."

36

That ancient and dilapidated motor car, with chaff on the floor of it, and the springs emerging from the seats, was waiting at Windwood to carry them to Bezill.

"Hallo, Mr Fulalove," said Herbert.

"Good afternoon, Master 'erbert," replied Mr Fulalove. "Good afternoon, sir," he said to Pellerin, with a nod of his head. He took two cases, and dumped them beside his seat in the front.

They drove in silence.

Would he find Mrs Shakeshaft (he refused to think of her as Mrs Gayfere) in widow's weeds? Of course, if he was honest, he would stop all this solemnity and begin laughing—yes, laughing. As he thought of laughing—laughing for joy—a sad smile crept round his lips. He'd not been a bad fellow, Gayfere. Life at Bezill would have been infinitely duller without him. Where would she hide now? His return was his triumph, a somewhat dismal sort of triumph, perhaps, but a triumph nevertheless. Should he declare his passion? He'd never actually done that. The voice of the custom official came back to him, "Have you anything to declare?"

"Only my passion."

The stubborn tower of Bezill came in sight. Had he overplayed his hand with Herbert? No. The boy was all right.

They entered the house and Herbert ran on to greet his mother and doubtless tell her of his adventures.

Wales came up to Pellerin.

"Tell me," said Pellerin, "what did Mr Gayfere die of?"

"He had a stroke, sir."

"When?"

"On the night of the wedding, I think, sir." He was conscious of a feeling of lightness, of relief. He'd only done Gayfere some good. A man in his condition needs quietening down. The bromide had done that. Why, he might have saved his life . . .

37

The cluster of tiny tombstones amid the trees reminded him of Gayfere. He imagined him buried here, alongside the mortal remains of Toby and Fido and Sue. Where is your bark now?

As he walked back to the house, he scanned the four windows of Mrs Shakeshaft's bedroom, hoping to see her peeping out.

She's hiding from me; this is absurd.

It occurred to him that she need never appear again; she could become a recluse in her own house—it was large enough to conceal one frightened woman—but how about hunting? Was she going to give that up? He did not think this possible.

While Herbert was trying on his father's helmet, with its handsome plume, and dropping the breast plate upon the floor, Pellerin was turning over the pages of an album of photographs. He recognized one Prime Minister and two Foreign Secretaries, guests at Bezill apparently.

He and Herbert were up in the tower. There was no Gayfere to disturb them now. Pellerin had taken in the view of the surrounding countryside, and seen at close range a kestrel in flight. He was feeling like an usurper king—at any moment, he feared, Mrs Gayfere would appear, and kick him down. *I'm the queen of the castle, get down you dirty rascal.*

He'd come up here to please Herbert (who was now losing himself in his father's enormous cavalry boots), and to find out what there was to find out.

Mrs Shakeshaft had had a tremendous row with her husband who was having an affair with her sister, Marion. Oh, well, that sort of thing went on even in the best of families.

Now here was a photograph of Herbert's father at Eton. And here he was at Sandhurst with other gentlemen cadets.

"That's Aunt Marion," said Herbert as the page fell open at the photograph of a young woman with light, sad eyes and a fluffy dog in her arms.

A pretty woman. How could one tell, from that dreamy face, that one day she'd go off her rocker, and stay off it, in spite of all the king's psychiatrists to get her back again. No smiler, she, but what was there to smile about?

"So that's Aunt Marion," said Pellerin.

Herbert drew the fearsome sword from its scabbard and pointed it at his tutor.

Pellerin, undaunted, turned the pages. At any moment he would fall dead for prizing open these secrets.

The girls' cricket eleven, Aunt Marion among them. A stalwart lot, they. Their names were printed below. Marion Shakeshaft . . .

Pellerin paused, and his head went up a couple of inches. Shakeshaft? That was a mistake, surely? Or was she a Shakeshaft? Impossible.

Oh, well, incest was not unheard of, even in the best of families. Far worse horrors had been committed in these days. He'd probably given her a baby. Careless fellow. No wonder she'd gone off her rocker . . .

Pellerin closed the album with a slam. He wanted to get out of this place, lock the door, never come back.

And what had happened to the baby, if there had been one? Come to think of it, Herbert didn't look like his mother at all. Pellerin opened the album again, hurriedly turned the pages till he found the photograph of Miss Marion Shakeshaft with her fluffy dog. Yes, Herbert did look extraordinarily like her ... Did it matter? Pellerin found himself looking at his pupil with critical apprehension.

But they had been quarrelling when Herbert was four years old ... Well, of course, Captain Shakeshaft could have continued the liaison in secret. He'd been forgiven once, perhaps twice, and Alice had adopted the baby, but like the dog that returneth to its vomit ... Pellerin heard the dim reverberation of Gayfere's voice: "You *must* divorce him. A man who will sleep with his sister, who will persist in sleeping with his sister, will do anything." But Captain Shakeshaft had saved them the trouble of divorcing him, and his sister had gone clean off her rocker.

Poor boy. He must never know. Never, never, never, never! No wonder he wrote poetry and had fits.

Suddenly he saw Mrs Gayfere in a new light. She was as cold as an ice lolly, but it was not surprising. Who wouldn't be as cold as an ice lolly in the circumstances? As cold as the cold winds of hell.

Wales brought him a letter. It was unstamped, and had not come through the post. It was, in fact, from Mrs Gayfere. Enclosed was a cheque. Pellerin noticed the cheque first of all. Then he read the letter. It was brief, but to the point.

His appointment as tutor to Herbert was terminated. Mrs Gayfere had dispensed with his services, and requested that he should leave Bezill at his earliest convenience. "As soon as possible, that is," Pellerin murmured to himself.

He rang for Wales.

"When is the next train to London?"

"In an hour's time, sir."

"I will catch it." Pellerin's decision was a sensible one, pregnant with promise for the future. Yes, he could do that, if a car was available to take him to the station.

Wales must have anticipated this, for he said immediately and (Pellerin thought) with relief, "The car will be waiting for you, sir."

"Where is Herbert?" asked Pellerin. He must speak to Herbert, say good-bye to him. Warm handshake and cheerful remarks. He could not defy Mrs Gayfere, tell her firmly, "I am *not* going. You can stand on your head, but I am *not* going. Do you understand? I am *not* going. *Not*. Now stand on your head." She who paid the piper, called the time, and she *had* paid the piper—the lot. He ran his finger along the serrated edge of the cheque. Yes, it was a cheque all right, and on beautiful blue paper, too. All cheques should be on beautiful blue paper.

Wales was hesitating. "He's not in the house, sir," he said at last.

"Where has he gone to?" There was no mistaking Pellerin's tone. This was a demand. Answer or fall dead.

A pause. "I am not permitted to say, sir," said Wales sorrowfully.

"Well, I like that. Can't I even say good-bye to the boy?"

Wales was at a loss for words.

The young manservant carried his suitcase and his typewriter to the waiting car. As Pellerin was about to step inside, Wales said, "I'm sorry you're going sir."

"Thank you, Wales. I'm sorry, too."

"Good-bye, sir."

Pellerin breathed a deep sigh, grunted good-bye, and stepped inside the car. Wales closed the door and the chauffeur drove off.

Oh, stop!

Almost an accident. His hair would be under the wheel.

Flowing hair—a youth in need of a haircut—Herbert!—had burst from the trees into the drive, waving his arms. The car was forced to slow down, and stop.

Herbert rushed up to the window. Pellerin immediately lowered it.

"I just wanted to say good-bye," he said.

There were tears in his eyes.

"Wait a minute," said Pellerin to the chauffeur, and got out.

They walked together amid the trees.

"Mama said I mustn't speak to you again," said Herbert. "She's mad with you. But I had to say good-bye." He paused, and then added, "Will you forgive me?"

"For what, Herbert?"

"For getting you the sack."

"How?"

"Through taking you up to the tower, of course. She found out. It was all my fault. I suppose one of the servants told her."

"It doesn't matter. I have to go to London, anyhow."

"I shall miss you."

"And I, you, Herbert."

"We had some good times together!" There was a glow of happiness amid his sorrow.

"Yes," said Pellerin, "we have had some good times and good adventures." He wondered if Herbert was thinking of anything in particular. "You'll have more good times in the future." He paused. "I hope you will like your new tutor."

"He won't be like you," said Herbert sadly.

"No, perhaps not."

They walked in silence for a while.

"I've been thinking," said Herbert slowly, "of . . ." He hesitated. ". . . of that girl in Lisbon."

"Do you mean the little lady with the horse-tail hair-style?"

"Yes," said Herbert, his cheeks growing red.

"Nice little girl. Kind."

"Oh, yes, very kind."

And then, with a rush, he came out with it.

"I love her, I want to marry her. Now that I have money of my own, do you think she would . . . would marry me?" Without waiting for an answer, he hurried on. "I want to go back to Lisbon at once, and beg her to marry me. I love her, I can't get her out of my mind. I have written these poems to her." He took from his inside pocket a sheaf of papers, close written, Poems to his Love.

Pellerin was at a loss for words. "I think," he said at last, "that you are a very nice person, Herbert." He glanced back towards Bezill, to the woman who was hidden there, a woman as cold as an ice lolly. But it was not her fault she was so cold!

"But Herbert, marriage is ..." It was no good. He couldn't go on. And unless he hurried off, he'd miss his train. "I think, Herbert, that you must do what you think is right and proper."

"But is it not right and proper that we should get married?" he asked, his frank face flushed with emotion. "Because of what happened between us, I mean."

"Oh, Herbert, I don't know," said Pellerin unhappily. "The world is full of illusions." He turned again towards the house and Mrs Gayfere, twice a widow. "You must do what you think is right, Herbert."

He put out his hand and Herbert grasped it. "Good-bye, Herbert!" Upon an impulse, he put his arms round him, and kissed him on the cheek. They clung to each other for a moment, and then, releasing him, Pellerin hurried back to the car.

"Good-bye! Good-bye!"

The boy's farewell rang in his ears as the car drove off.

THE END

Lightning Source UK Ltd.
Milton Keynes UK
UKHW020003221022
410730UK00024B/344